Murder in Bemidji

...Or

Paul's Bloody Trousers

D1566913

MURDER IN BEMIDJI

...OR...

PAUL'S BLOODY TROUSER

GERALD ANDERSON

NORTH STAR PRESS OF ST. CLOUD, INC.
St. Cloud, Minnesota

In memory of my beautiful soul-mate, best friend, and wife:
Barbara
1950-2011

ISBN-13: 978-0-87839-565-1

First Edition, September 1, 2011

Printed in the United States of America

Published by
North Star Press of St. Cloud, Inc.
P.O. Box 451
St. Cloud, Minnesota 56302

northstarpress.com

Murder in Bemidji

... Or

Paul's Bloody Trousers

Prologue

L ET US CALL THEM, FOR NOW, "MURDERER," AND "VICTIM." Victim stood in the shadows behind the giant blue ox. It was eerily silent. The only sounds came from a few ripples gently lapping onto the shore of Lake Bemidji and, in the distance, exhaust fumes drifted through the air from a passing tanker on Highway 2. The fury of the thunderstorm system that had ripped across northern Minnesota five hours earlier left hundreds of small puddles on the tarred surface of the parking lot, which now reflected the light from a distant street lamp. In the east, flashes of lightning illuminated a sky indifferent to the violence that would soon occur in this vacation paradise.

It was now 1:40 a.m., and murderer was already ten minutes late for the appointment. Victim held his breath and his position for too long. He relaxed slightly and shifted his weight onto his other leg while slowly exhaling, and tried to control his breathing. For the hundredth time in the last fifteen minutes, he frantically looked in all directions. Perhaps his antagonist wouldn't come. He began to take long regular breaths and his heart slowed down. He began to hope that, after all, the appointment would not be kept. Maybe it was madness after all. Was it his place to play avenging angel? He noticed that he was no longer gripping the hunting knife with the determination that he had when he had first taken his position. When he thought about it now, he wondered if he really would have had the courage to kill. He decided, "If that vermin does come, I'll just stage a confrontation. I'll tell all I know in such a way that there will be no way for him to deny it. Then I'll show my knife and tell him that his 'miserable life isn't worth taking! Let the law take its course. Let the shame and humiliation be shared by your family.' Yeah, that's what I'll do."

Victim heard a noise to his left. He had a brief panic attack as he tried to see through the gloom. He heard it again. In possession of his nerves once more, he peered close to the ground and saw a tiny gleam. It was the eye of a chipmunk. He had been totally unnerved by a chipmunk. "Well," Victim thought, "if I'm scared of a chipmunk, it's time I quit and went to bed." He smiled as the little rodent scurried away and put his knife away in its sheath.

His smile remained as the knife, held in a hand covered by a rubber glove, cut right across his throat. He was puzzled at first, because nothing seemed to hurt, and he was gushing blood. He grasped his neck and blood spurted through his fingers. Murderer then pushed the knife deep into his chest and left it there. Murderer smiled into the dying eyes and said simply, "Surprise!!"

Victim stumbled a few feet and grabbed the only support available. It was the right leg of a giant pair of blue concrete trousers. The trousers turned very red.

CHAPTER ONE

"I T JUST DOESN'T GET MUCH BETTER than this! Aren't you glad that you are a Minnesotan? Look at that!" the sheriff of Otter Tail County said as he put his arm around his slightly chubby wife and together they gazed across the lake. It was ten-thirty on the evening of June 21st, the longest day of the year. It was still light to the northwest, and the glassy surface of Lake Itasca reflected magenta-colored fleecy clouds. In the dimming twilight they walked along a trail under a canopy of pines. The trail was soft, capreted by pine needles, so that not even their footsteps made a sound. Suddenly, from a nearby inlet, they heard the eerie wail of a loon.

For a time, it seemed almost sacrilegious to speak, then finally Ellie took her husband's hand and snuggled under his arm and sighed, "I'm so glad we decided to do this. I have wanted to stay at Douglas Lodge since I first saw it in fifth grade. It took me fifty years to do it, but it was worth the wait." Silently, and with mutual accord, they slowly began walking back to the lodge along Dr. Robert's Trail.

Douglas Lodge, on the south shore of Lake Itasca, was built in 1905 in the "rustic style." Oldest building in Itasca State Park, it was the first to accommodate guests. Built out of peeled red pine logs harvested from the surrounding forest, it was named after William B. Douglas, a Minnesota attorney general instrumental in the conservation movement. The interior of the two-story building included a large reception room with a beautifully crafted stone fireplace. No television here, just old books, new paperbacks, jigsaw puzzles,

3

and game boards. Around the main building were other cabins of a more rustic nature without the full amenities. It was the full amenities that appealed to the couple who signed in as Mr. and Mrs. P. Knutson, Fergus Falls, Minnesota.

As they left behind their solitude and emerged into the halo of light coming from the lodge, Palmer said, "I don't remember, did you ever take geology in college?" Ellie, somewhat surprised, said, "No, and I don't remember much of what I learned in high school. How so?"

"I did take geology at good old Fergus Falls State University. I didn't want to, but I had to take a science for general education, the biology class was full and I was afraid of chemistry and physics. I liked it. You know, they used to think all of these Minnesota lakes were leftovers from the great flood—you know, Noah and all that. Anyhow, I had this professor who explained the whole thing in terms of ice locks from the age of glaciers, the great ice tunnels that ran under the glaciers and led to the eventual formation of ancient Lake Agassiz—which, as you may know, was larger than all of the great lakes put together. This was a 'knob and kettle' region. The 'knobs' were mounds of dirt and gravel scraped up at the end of the glacier, and the 'kettles' were areas where large pieces of ice were left under the surface. A few thousand years later, you have hills and ten thousand Minnesota lakes. It also explains the formation of the Lake Itasca basin, and consequently, the birth of the Mississippi River."

"And you remember all that from college?" Ellie asked, as she flashed admiring blue eyes at her husband. "Were you thinking of that this afternoon when we took off our shoes and waded across the 'Mighty Mississip'?"

"Matter of fact, I was," her husband admitted. "But I was also thinking how much I enjoyed being able to wander around wearing shorts. Apparently cops wear shorts in the

Southwest all the time, and nobody thinks anything of it. If I wore shorts in any place but my back yard, it would raise eyebrows. But that would be so cool. And they don't have to be khaki colored either. These are nice!"

As they climbed the stairs to their room at the Douglas Lodge, Ellie observed Palmer's maroon-and-green-plaid shorts and silently questioned the benefits of moving to the Southwest. They closed the door and lay down on the bed. Ellie propped her somewhat plump body up on one elbow and gazed at Palmer with her green eyes. "Do remember the first time you came to Itasca?" She asked.

"Yah," Palmer replied, with a smile. He moved his round bifocals to rest on the edge of his receding hairline and said, "I was, I don't know, maybe about eight at the time, I guess. We crossed the river just as we did this afternoon. My parents wanted my brother Rolf to lead me across, but he refused—I think he thought it was too much of a kid thing—so my mother took off her shoes and led me across. That big log sign was there then, too, telling everyone that from that very spot the Mississippi begins a 2,552 mile journey to the Gulf of Mexico. Well, that made a big impression on me. One of the books I read in third grade had been about a sea captain, and I wanted to see the ocean. You know, other than from the window of an airplane, I still haven't seen the ocean. We've gotta go there when I retire," he said while putting both hands behind his head, stretched out on the bed, and sighed.

"And when will that be, Palmer?"

"Maybe sooner than you think. Did I tell you about Neal Meyer? The sheriff of Beltrami County? The one who is supposed to host the conference tomorrow?"

"What about him?" Ellie asked with her forehead wrinkling in concern.

"He announced last week that he was retiring, effective immediately. Since I'm on the program tomorrow, he called me up to tell me. It seems he has cancer. Now, apparently, it's not fatal, not yet anyway, but he's going to have to have surgery in a few weeks and that will take a while to recover from. Then he starts talking about all the places he and his wife planned to go 'before it was too late.' Anyhow, it made me think. I'm not getting any younger."

It made Ellie uncomfortable to hear Palmer talk about that kind of subject, perhaps because it reminded her of her own mortality. She tried to redirect the subject, "What else do you remember from your first trip to Itasca?"

"Well, things were different then, you know," Palmer said wistfully. "There was no sensitivity to Native Americans at all, for one thing. I remember that just a few yards from the head-waters someone had put up a canvas teepee and they had this guy dressed up in the full regalia of an Indian chief. And, of course, you could have your picture taken with him."

"Did your parents take a picture of you with him?" Ellie asked, suppressing a giggle.

"Of course. Rolf and I stood on either side of Chief Thun-dercloud or whatever they called him. I wonder if Rolf still has that picture? Anyway, they sold genuine Indian sou-venirs, more than likely made in Japan in those days, and my dad bought me a little bow and arrow set. The arrows were tipped with rubber suction cups. Just like the Indians used! I loved it. I gotta tell that story to Jason Two Bears."

"Who's Jason Two Bears?"

"He's a Native American, an Ojibwe."

"Well, yes, I sort of figured that out all by myself. Two Bears isn't exactly your standard Norwegian last name. But who is Two Bears?"

"Oh, he is, or was, the chief deputy of Sheriff Meyer. Bright guy. I doubt if Two Bears is over thirty years old. Neal told me that he is going to be the acting sheriff until the next election. I met him at last year's Northwestern Minnesota

Association of County Sheriffs meeting in Crookston. I'll introduce him to you tomorrow night. You'll like him."

Palmer loosened his shoes and let them fall one by one to the floor, much to the annoyance of the couple from Chicago in the room below. Palmer and Ellie took turns performing their evening ablutions and snuggled between the crisp sheets of a surprisingly comfortable bed. When Palmer turned out the lights, Ellie said, "Would you run something by me once again? What is this conference all about? Remember, this is the first one you have ever taken me to."

"Yah, well," Palmer began, with a little trepidation in his voice. The room was dark, with only a faint glimmer of starlight coming from the window. "It's not like I've tried to keep you away from them. I mean, for most of the existence of the conference, you really wouldn't have enjoyed it. In the first place, it was all stag. 'No women allowed' may not have appeared in any by-laws, but it was the unwritten rule. At least, it was until Jeannie Beare was elected sheriff of Polk County.

Then, of course, since Polk County is one of the largest counties in the state, you couldn't leave her out, so everything changed, including the venue. As you may recall, we used to meet at the Grundorf Pines Resort. This was located on Lake Grundorf, a mile south of Grundorf, the county seat of Green County. Well, 'dorf' means 'town' in German, and 'grun' means 'green'—"Greentown"—so you might figure that it is a German community. Nothing could be farther from the truth. James J.—you could never leave out the 'J' —Green was a Yankee merchant who had done very well indeed by supplying the union army with hay for their horses. He noticed that there was still timber in Minnesota that Weyerhauser had not yet managed to steal. He worked out some kind of understanding with James J. Hill—by the way, there is some speculation that Green's middle initial was not J at all, but was a transparent attempt to be associated with Hill, the Empire Builder. So, old man Green tries to make a German sounding village appealing to German immigrants and at the same time slyly naming a town after himself. Furthermore, since hardly anyone lived up there, not counting the Indians, and, of course, nobody did count them in those days, Green was able to supply a few needy state senators with a few dollars and, whambo-flusho! there's a county named after him."

"Hmmm," Ellie said, her social conscience alerted. "Sounds like a perfect capitalistic exploiter."

"Actually, he may have been the best of the family. Very few Germans ever came to Grundorf, Minnesota, but after the Russian tsar began to oppress the Finns, a lot of them wanted to come to Minnesota at any cost. Those guys could sling an axe and were just what Green was looking for. For a time, the town did prosper from its Green Sawmill, Green General Store, and the magnificent Green Hotel. About this time, old James J. shuffled off his mortal coil and his son Benjamin took over. All he had to do was to continue what his old man had put in motion. Naturally, and inevitably, it didn't take too much time before those hardworking Finns had cut down all the pines and the Greens never even considered reforestation—a bit of irony that Al Gore would appreciate, I mean, hardly part of the "green" revolution. Anyhow, without the forest covering, erosion destroyed what was left. The Ojibwe, who depended on the fragile ecological balance, faced ruination and many were forced to leave. Somebody told me that many of the people who live on the Red Lake reservation once lived in Green County.

In any event, in 1919 the Spanish flu carried away the not particularly missed Benjamin Green and the fate of the county was in the hands of Graham Green, or Grammy Green, as he was called. There are plenty of stories about him. He was a shiftless character who may have murdered his brother. I don't know if that part is true, but the mere fact that it can be repeated tells you something about how he was regarded. By this time, the timber was all gone, the sawmill was closed, and the general store was losing money because the town had lost half of its population. Grammy Green spent his time in the hotel or out on the lake. Now, Lake Grundorf was one heck of a lake for walleye. Grammy began to notice that some people came to stay in the hotel just to go fishing. In the prosperous and "roaring" twenties, this was enough to keep him going. Then came the Great Depression. Now here is where the family fortune was made."

"In the Depression? How so?"

"Ah, well, look at the map. You may notice that a small part of the county is on the shore of Lake of the Woods. What's on the northern shore? Canada. What does Canada have?"

"Um, sensible gun laws, universal health care, decent public transportation?"

"Yah, yah, yah, and hockey players and mounties—but I'm talking about 1930. Put it this way. What don't they have? They don't have prohibition. I suppose you can see where this is going."

"Elliot Ness and the boys? The Untouchables? Robert Stack and Kevin Costner?"

"Sort of, except no law ever got to Grammy Green. Boats were soon crossing the lake filled with rye whiskey, gin, and vodka—not so much beer, not enough profit per ounce for Grammy. Grundorf became prosperous almost overnight. Booze was taken down to the rail yard in Bemidji where a few carefully bribed workers put it into a box car that was made to look like it was carrying paint. Right! I mean, gallons of paint originating in Bemidji! The "paint" boxcar would find its way to a siding just outside St. Paul. Major money, major organization. Anyway, it took the small truckers the better part of a day to haul the booze down to Bemidji and go back again, and they needed a place to stay, so there was a little housing boom. The general store started making money again. With that element in town, well, they had to be entertained somehow, didn't they? In the Grundorf 'speakeasies' there was no reason to speak easy. There was gambling and prostitution, so the money just kept pouring in. They say John Dillinger had a special room in the hotel, but he wanted something better. So you know what Grammy did?"

"What?" asked Ellie, now totally caught in the story.

"He decided it was time to build up a resort on the shores of beautiful Lake Grundorf. By this time, everyone knew that the end was in sight for Herbert Hoover and his policies and Roosevelt let it be known that if he became president he would end prohibition. Well, where's the profit in transporting booze legally through the most distant town in the state? But, if the depression ended and people wanted to do a little high class fishing, and since the town still had a reputation for at least a little fun, well, the entrepreneurship that had been dormant in Grammy Green for so long was now at last unleashed.

"So that's where you had your meetings? The Grundorf Pines Resort? I presume the 'prostitution' problem had long since been eradicated," said Ellie, with a sniff.

"You presume wrong," said Palmer. "Of course it is against the law. But the law has to be enforced. And this is where Harvey Green comes in.

"You see," he continued, relishing the story, "Grammy Green had two sons, Harley and Harvey. Harley, the older one, seemed to have a little flair for inn-keeping and gradually took over for Grammy—who lived to be ninety-three, by the way, morally and physically so crooked that he could hide behind a cork-screw. Well, what to do with Harvey? By the nineteen-sixties, the county was rapidly losing population. Grundorf is the county seat and that has barely eleven hundred people in it. There are only a few other towns in the whole county and most of the land is swampland. The few decent lakes that do exist are too remote to be profitable sites for resorts. Harvey did go down to Bemidji State College, as it was called then, for a couple of quarters, where he apparently majored in beer drinking and smoking grass. He eventually flunked out and returned home. I don't think he is particularly stupid—he does seem to have an air of animal cunning about him—but he is chronically lazy.

"Well, nobody said, certainly at that time, that you had to be able to read, let alone have a degree, to be a county sheriff. With the aid of his father, who could twist the arm of every citizen in the county, Harvey was elected county sheriff. This, by the way, got a certain amount of press in the Cities—you know, 'Bootlegger's Son Now County Sheriff'— but everybody got tired of that story before too long, and it was just too remote to bother anybody in St. Paul.

"And so it went. The county kept losing people, and it didn't make sense to have both a county auditor and a county treasurer so those positions were combined. And then, they discovered they could save even more money if they combined those positions with that of county sheriff. They now call the Green County Courthouse simply 'Harvey House.' He has a secretary, apparently quite compliant and quite good looking, and three dull normal doughnut-stuffed deputies. Somehow, and this is something I don't know for sure, but there was some talk about this a while ago, all those staff cuts did not result in a lower budget. All this means is that Harvey Green can let his brother Harley get by with whatever he wants at the resort. You know how we always had a set weekend for our sheriffs' conference? We finally figured out that he held it the weekend before the fishing opener so that he could use that weekend to train his staff for the summer. He still charged the various county sheriffs a nice, albeit reduced, price to stay there. The kitchen staff learned the ropes at our expense. Nobody really cared. There was a lot of beer and a lot of Jim Beam. I never saw any girls, but I heard that a couple of the guys did go into town one night. Some guys even did some illegal fishing. They never even bothered to buy a license. I mean, here we are, having taken an oath, and . . . Ellie?"

A long sonorous intake of air came from Ellie's partially opened mouth. It had, after all, been a very long day. Neither of them were used to all that fresh air. Palmer stared out of the window at the incredibly bright stars, wishing he had not decided to play history teacher. He extended his foot to just the right place on Ellie's leg and gave a shove, not hard enough to wake her, but, as he had learned over the last thirty years, enough to get her to roll over and stop snoring. He puffed up his pillow and was soon dreaming about shooting rubber-tipped arrows.

CHAPTER TWO

PERHAPS THE MOST MARVELOUS THING ABOUT STAYING at Douglas Lodge is the opportunity to have a breakfast fit for a lumberjack. A voice in the back of Palmer's mind screamed warnings about cholesterol, but he was soon slapping butter on the pancakes and drooling over the sausages. The coffee was great and the morning air was crisp. They didn't have to check into the Bemidji Paul Bunyan Radisson until later in the day, so they decided to make the best of their time in Itasca. Founded in 1891 by the Minnesota Legislature, it was only the second state park created in the United States, trailing only Niagara Falls. Within the thirty-two thousand acres of parkland are one hundred and fifty-seven lakes, including the lake determined to be the true source of the Mississippi. Discovered by Henry Rowe Schoolcraft in 1832, after several other expeditions had failed, he named the lake by combining the Latin words for "truth" and "head." From *veritas caput* came "Itasca."

To get a good look at it, Palmer and Ellie checked out of the Douglas Lodge and hiked to the Aiton Heights Fire Tower. After a climb that had Palmer concerned about the availability of emergency cardiac equipment, they viewed the park from the one-hundred-foot summit.

Later, they drove to Preacher's Grove. In the 1920s a conference of preachers was held under the spreading canopy of red pines. While not quite in the league of the giant redwoods of California, the red pines of Preacher's Grove are still in their natural state and some of the trees are almost three hundred years old. As they made their way along the path to the lake,

Palmer could not help looking up to see clouds of green pine needles obscuring the blue sky. "Preacher's Grove," Palmer thought, "is a swell name for this place. If anyone ever wanted to wax eloquent on God's creation, this would be the cathedral in which to do it." As they reached the lake and prepared to sit on the log bench, Ellie noticed a chipmunk. "Look, he's been saving a place for us," she said.

For the rest of the morning, they kept their eyes peeled for any of the two hundred bird species that make their home in Itasca, and thrilled to the sight of a bald eagle gliding over the lake. There is archeological evidence of visitors eight thousand years ago at the Bison Kill Site, dating back to the Early Eastern Archaic period. There are also two visitor centers, with modern interpretive displays to serve the demands of the half million modern visitors who come to Itasca every year.

But it was time to go. Palmer was going to be the featured speaker that night at the Northwestern Minnesota Association of County Sheriff's Conference. He needed to spend some time looking over his notes and practicing his speech, which, in the printed program, was titled "The Value of Tax-Funded Law Enforcement at the County Level for the Twenty-First Century." He needed an introduction, something to get everyone's attention, but as he directed his Acura TL north on state Highway 2 the classic rock station presented "American Woman," by Winnipeg's finest, The Guess Who. Palmer was soon singing along with "gotta get away, gotta get away . . ." The music moved him, the speedometer climbed and the thirty-one miles passed quickly.

❋ ❋

BEMIDJI MINNESOTA IS LOCATED NINETY MILES SOUTH of Rainy River, Ontario, and two-hundred eleven miles northwest of

Minneapolis. With a population of over 13,000, it is about the same size as Palmer's beloved Fergus Falls. It is, however, a quite different city. Fergus Falls is surrounded by wheat fields, dairy farms, and a lot of lakes, but Bemidji is surrounded by swamps, timber, and larger, deeper lakes. People who live in Fergus Falls hope that others will visit their fair town, but the people of Bemidji depend on it. Scores of resorts are to be found on lakes such as Plantagenet Lake, Turtle Lake, Three Island Lake, and dozens more. The largest lake in the area is Lake Bemidji and the city is located on the beautiful southern shore. Bemidji State University, on the northern edge of the city, can lay claim to one of the most gorgeous university settings in the nation.

Palmer and Ellie checked into room 418 of the Radisson Paul Bunyan, located just across Bemidji Avenue from one of the most famous statues in America. It is said (and this would be very hard to prove or disprove, so most people are comfortable in believing it) that the statue of Paul Bunyan (together with, Babe, the Blue Ox) is the second most photographed statue in the United States, trailing only the Statue of Liberty. Paul was made of concrete in 1937, and is eighteen feet tall. There is speculation that the real Paul Bunyan was larger.

Mr. and Mrs. Knutson dropped their single suitcase on the bed of their room and went out on the balcony to admire the view. Lake Bemidji looked like a tourist poster. Several sailboats glided along the near the shore and not far away from the resort, a speedboat pulled two water skiers. The sun danced off the water as the cool breeze reached all the way to their fifth floor room. Down below, Palmer spotted "Paul's Pancake House," Paul Bunyan Dry Cleaners," "Bunyan Lanes," and "Babe's Oxburgers"—home of the famous Blue Ox burger, a half-pound of ground beef marbled with blue cheese. The most classy, however, was "Paul Bunyan's

Bait and Tackle Shop," with a telephone pole stuck into the ground at a ninety degree angle. A barrel had been bolted onto the pole, with a thick rope wound around it and then extended to the top. From there, the rope dangled down with a red-and-white-painted basketball affixed—to serve as a bobber—and ending in a gaudy fishing lure. "Paul Bunyan's Rod and Reel." Now really, what kind of snob would not find that charming?

"Too bad we have to eat our supper at that banquet," Palmer said, squinting from the sun's rays. "There's supposed to be a pretty good German restaurant here and a good Italian restaurant, too. I suppose it would not look good if we skipped the banquet meal and showed up just for the speech."

"No, I don't think that would be appreciated," Ellie agreed. "although since you are the keynote speaker, they could hardly start things without you. Tell me more about tonight. I think I missed a few details last night. I was paying attention, you know, it was just that, well, you have this soothing voice. Perhaps you should put a little more zip into your delivery tonight. The last thing I remember you telling me about was how the conference always used to held at the Grundorf Pines Resort. How long has it been since you were there?"

"I think it's been at least ten years, because that's about as long as we have had women sheriffs in this part of the state. The way it works now is that it is a revolving thing. Speaking of that, um, I suppose I should have mentioned this before, but I didn't want you to get all 'organizational' on me."

"What? What did you volunteer me to do now?" Ellie asked suspiciously.

"Well, I volunteered to host the conference in Fergus Falls next summer. This will not involve you at all. I've already had my secretary doing all the reservations at the Holliday Inn. But that's just why I didn't tell you. You always have to act the hostess."

"Well, dah! If you are going to be the host, I automatically become the hostess. You men always think it is so simple. How many people do you expect to come to Fergus Falls?"

"Well, I suppose about the same number as will be here in Bemidji. Maybe more because it is easier to get to since Fergus Falls is on the interstate, but maybe less since Bemidji is more of a resort town. Last year we held it in Thief River Falls. That's a pretty town, but it is kind off the beaten track, so I think we only had about thirty people show up. I would think we should have about forty tonight. The biggest conference is always when we have it in Moorhead. Of course, you're looking at a metropolitan area of about 165,000 people, so that brings in all the wives and a few extra deputies and everybody drifts off to go shopping or to the museums or to the restaurants. We also usually get some students from the criminal justice departments at North Dakota State University and Minnesota State University Moorhead, to say nothing of all the sociology students from Concordia College. In fact, I've made a couple of calls, and I think I'm going to be able to get this guy from NDSU to be our banquet speaker."

"So, you've been cooking up this whole thing for a year and decided not to tell me about it?"

"Er, um, yah, I guess I have."

"Men! What do you say we take our camera and go down to visit Paul and Babe. I'll take your picture holding Paul's hand. I'll bet that won't be the first time for you."

"No," Palmer agreed, "my mother had to take my picture with Paul every time we went through town. It's kind of funny. By the time I was a teenager, he didn't seem so tall anymore."

They crossed Bemidji Avenue and Ellie searched for the perfect vantage point. Palmer self-consciously reached up and took Paul's hand. Ellie took three or four digital shots just to make sure she got a good one, then Palmer made Ellie hold Paul's hand while he took one. Ellie said, "You can take more than one, you know. It's not like we have to take the film into the drugstore anymore. What if your picture made me look fat? By the way, does Paul look just like you remembered him?"

"I guess so, but look how bright blue Babe is and how Paul's red plaid coat looks so neat. They must have repainted this spring. I seem to recall that there were always a few chunks of concrete missing. There used to be a little amusement park for little kids connected with this thing. Look, in the grass over there. You can still see the old tracks of that little train that they had. I used to love that thing. I suppose the guy who ran it is long gone by now, and I suppose insurance liability is such that they could never run a little thing like that anymore. Kind of sad, really. What's that building over there?"

As they got closer to the modern building, Ellie said, "The sign says that it is the Bemidji Tourist Information Center. Let's go see. Unless, that is, you want to go over your speech some more."

"I really should," Palmer agreed, "but it wouldn't hurt to take a peek, I suppose."

Inside the center there was an information desk and several artifacts from the life of Paul Bunyan, including a gigantic toothbrush, a pair of incredibly large baby moccasins, a huge wallet, a safety pin for baby Paul's diapers, and scissors. Apparently there had never been an attempt to keep all of the articles in scale, that would be too nitpicking and no one was in the mood to do that. When they reached outside, they noticed that the temperature and humidity had risen to uncomfortable levels, so the Knutsons retired to the coolness of their hotel room.

Palmer leaned back on the bed with his arms behind his head. "You know, maybe we should stay here until Sunday. They celebrate the Swedish Midsommar festival then. Now, you know how I feel about Swedes, but they really do have a nice tradition for a mid-summer celebration. I remember as a kid my folks would take us to that Swedish church in the country, not too far from our farm. It was held the Sunday closest to the summer solstice. They had a big church dinner, usually ham or meatballs, as I recall, and then everyone would lay around digesting the food. The kids usually played a softball game in the pasture next to the church; that was always fun. And then they had a concessions stand. They hauled out a freezer from the creamery in Underwood and they would have three different kinds of ice cream—vanilla, chocolate, and strawberry, naturally—and they would also have this big tub of ice and they sold pop. I think it cost a nickel, or maybe a dime and they sold candy and stuff, too. They also had a box of cigars there, so the men could buy a stogie. I'll never forget looking over and seeing my old man puffing on a cigar. I was shocked and I don't think my mother was all that pleased. Anyhow, after a while they would have a program, light on the preaching, but heavy on the singing, usually some of those old Swedish hymns that we also sang in the Norwegian church. All in all, it was something to look forward to. I mean, when you're a kid on the farm, you don't get much of a chance to play ball, sometimes they called it 'kittenball' instead of softball, I don't know if there was any difference. Yah, maybe those Swedes were all right."

Ellie recognized this as a major concession from Palmer. Of course, the only people who could tell the difference between a Swede and a Norwegian was another Swede or Norwegian. The general feeling among the Norwegians was that the Swedes were the worst possible ethnic group with the possible exception of everyone else. Palmer rested his eyes with a pleasant smile on his face.

CHAPTER THREE

I N ROOM 232 OF THE RADISSON PAUL BUNYAN, Brad Nichols, sheriff of Hayes County, toweled off his naked body, unconcerned with the fact that the drapes were wide open. Karen Nichols, similarly attired, emerged from the bathroom and gasped, "For heaven's sake, Brad, close the drapes. Somebody might see you!"

"Ah, so what? I doubt if anybody from Henjum has checked in. Nobody else knows us. Relax," Brad said calmly.

"I am not coming out until you close the drapes." The cords squeaked, the drapes closed, and Karen cautiously looked out. "That's better. Now you can mix me a nice drinkie-poo."

They had been swimming in the hotel pool. Swimming in a lake was no particular treat for them, since they could do that any day. But lolling at a pool-side, sun bathing in anonymity, ah, that was the life. One kid staying with a friend, another kid at Boy Scout camp, they were alone at last. "Short one or a tall one?" Brad asked.

"What are you having?"

"What difference does it make to you?"

"All right, make me a tall one, too. But take it easy on that stuff. Isn't there supposed to be an open bar during the social hour before the banquet?"

"Sure, we can order a drink for five bucks. I prefer to be my own bartender," he said, as he unscrewed the cap off the large bottle of Gordon's Gin. "You did remember to stick a lime in the bag, didn't you?"

"Yes. Did you remember to bring your Swiss Army knife along to cut it with?"

Brad muttered a curse. He had just turned forty years old. There were a few streaks of gray in his light-brown hair and even more in his carefully trimmed mustache. He had gotten the job of sheriff at a relatively young age and grew the mustache because he thought it made him look more like an authority figure. It never did, of course, and now that it was rather out of fashion, his wife hinted that perhaps he should cut it off. He promised to do so, but hadn't quite gotten around to it. His fair skin, sunburned during the hour spent at the pool, set off his deep-blue eyes. He stuffed a boney hand into the ice bucket and filled two glasses.

After allowing him to wallow in his disappointment for a few minutes, Karen said, obviously pleased with herself, "Well, I did manage to remember the knife." She was a tall woman with naturally mousy hair smartened up with blonde accents and cut in a rather outdated shag. Her large brown eyes reflected keen intelligence, doubt, joy and eroticism, but Brad could never figure out which, at least, during the time in which it would have been most advantageous to him. She had a narrow body that was once too thin, then came the first child and she was too large, then thin again. Suffice it to say, she had a lot of clothes to meet any size. Wrapped in a towel and sitting on the bed, Brad decided that she was now just right.

They had arrived in mid-afternoon from Henjum, a town of about fifteen hundred people located on the edge of the prairie and the county seat of Hayes County. It was not a prosperous county. The land was fertile, although not as fertile as the counties in the Red River Valley, but over the years the town developed the same pattern as one found all across rural America. With increasing mechanization, the farms got bigger. Therefore, the tractors had to get bigger. One man could farm a lot more land and, in fact, he needed to if he were going to pay off that tractor. So he bought the farm next to him and then the farm next to that. The former residents retired or just quit farming and moved out of the county. The small towns got smaller. Were it not for a state subsidy, Hayes County would never have been able to pay its sheriff.

But they didn't pay him much. Year by year the salary slipped below the annual inflation rate and year by year his pay suffered in comparison to those more blessed law enforcement officers. So a free night in a Radisson was a much appreciated perk to the job. It was a job, moreover, that Brad Nichols liked and a job he could do well. It was something that he and Palmer Knutson had in common, and it was one of the reasons that brought him to the conference.

"I wonder how Palmer will take the whole award thing tonight," he said, as he handed Karen her drink. "He is so set in his modest, Lutheran self-effacing ways. I still think somebody should have told him. Who knows how he will react?"

"You mean," Karen asked, "it is a total surprise to him? Is that wise?"

"I don't know. But Neal Meyer—he's the sheriff here in Bemidji, or at least was up until a week ago—is a longtime friend of Palmer's. He's been plotting this for a year, and he was going to be the presenter until he suddenly decided to go to Canada. He set this whole thing up to make Palmer think he's at the head table because he is supposed to give a speech. Meyer had this plaque made up that recognizes Knutson as the Northwest Minnesota Sheriff of the Year."

"Oh," Karen said, after taking a long pull on her G and T. "Does that mean it will be an annual award?"

"Yeah, that's how it's suppose to work out. We'll form some kind of committee and each year we will pick the winner. Like Neal said, it will be good publicity and will not cost that much. Each year that somebody wins it gives his local paper something nice to write about him."

"Or her local paper?"

"Huh? Oh yeah, sure, we've got women sheriffs now. Ever since Marge Gunderson in the movie *Fargo*. I'm sure Jeanne Beare in Polk County will win it soon enough."

"Do you think you will win it one year, dear?"

"Yes, I do. We come from one of the smallest counties in the area, hardly any crime ever happens so no one ever hears about me, but if I learned anything from my dad it was that all you need to do is do your duty over the course of time and recognition will come. I'll never forget how proud he was at being named Rural Mail Carrier of the Year for the state of Minnesota. And when they gave him that award, my mom stood there and just beamed," Brad said before taking a drink.

For a few painful seconds two thoughts went through the mind of Karen Nichols. The first was a bitter idea that the best way they could use the award was for firewood to allay the cost of heating their house. The second was the somewhat uncomfortable realization that Brad was increasingly relying on county property to stretch out their income. Brad had not bought a stamp for personal use, for instance, in several years. However minor those transgressions may be, it was not the kind of thing that led to awards. Aloud she said, "Tell you what, Brad, you win and I'll be right up there beaming like your mom was. I think you're a great sheriff. Knutson got all that publicity for solving a few murders, but hey, if anybody got around to committing a murder in Hayes County, you could solve cases like that, too. And I'll tell you something else. If anybody wants to mess around with my sheriff, they'll have me to contend with."

Brad noticed that her towel was just about ready to fall off. Perhaps with a little help . . . but Karen was warming up to the topic.

"I keep thinking about the opportunity you had to be appointed assistant chief of police for Edina. We could have found a nice home in the suburbs, the kids could have gone to a really great school and the money would have been twice what you make now. But no, one nasty small town sheriff torpedoed that, didn't he?"

"Well, maybe," Brad's brow furrowed and his eyes hardened. "That's what we heard, but I suppose it could have been someone else. Still, you know, they might have hired some other guy anyway. It's just that, since then, I haven't really had a good shot at anything else. I mean, I like Henjum, it's a nice town and all that, but the job is a total dead end. I just wish that I could have had one fair shot at moving up."

Brad was young enough to keep on dreaming and poor enough to maintain secret fantasies of vengeance. Since the cutbacks on the budgets, he had been forced to handle more of the financial aspects of the county and well, who could blame him if he found a few ways to provide himself with a little extra reimbursement? Somebody must have been suspicious and started nosing around, and that nasty little knowledge had been used against him. It had to be that rotten Green, but could there be anybody else?

Karen took a monumental swig of gin and said, "So, is he going to be at the conference? Polluting the very air we breathe?"

A look of sadness and resignation came over Brad's face. "Yeah, I suppose he is. In fact I think I saw his car in the parking lot. It's hard to miss. It's got more paint and decals on it than any car you'll ever see. It looks like a cross between a circus wagon and a Nascar racing machine. But that's him, you know. He never cares about the well being of others. He only wants to scare them."

"You know, I would just like to see him get what he deserves. Now don't give me all that crap about due process of law and how one cannot take the law into one's own hands. But somebody really ought to murder that guy. Like they used to say on *Gunsmoke*, he's someone who just needs killin.' You've been in court. Can you imagine a jury convicting a person who rids the world of that vile creature?" Karen said, grinding her teeth.

Brad noticed that the towel was all but off, and didn't feel like continuing a pointless argument on the finer points of the law. He tried to bring the topic to a close. "Yes, juries convict people of killing vermin all the time. Besides, there is probably nothing else we have to fear from him. What more can he do? Remember, revenge never really accomplishes anything. Let's forget it and move on."

Oblivious to the position of the towel, Karen said, "I disagree. I think revenge serves a marvelous purpose. I'd feel very good if something bad happened to him."

It took some time and another "freshening up" of the gin and tonic, for Brad to get her into a much better mood.

* *

ALAN SORGREN AND HIS WIFE, CARLA, checked into room 317 on the third floor and dumped their bag in the corner. Carla opened the drapes and looked out. "Couldn't you have checked to see if we could get a room with a view of the lake? Look at this! Parking lots and railroad tracks! Lake Bemidji—6,420 acres and we can't see a drop of water. But, oh goodie, if I crane my neck and look up north, I can see the Paul Bunyan Mall. And, oh look! There's K-Mart."

Alan Sorgren, sheriff of Monroe County, ducked his head as he passed under the light fixture. It was not necessary, but at six-foot-six, it was a habit he had developed over time. Sorgren was the tallest sheriff in Minnesota, but not the best. Not that it mattered, since hardly any crime took place in Monroe County. Or, at least, hardly any that was actively investigated. It was rumored that Monroe County had the highest per-capita number of methamphetamine labs in the state, but since none were ever busted, it would appear that there was no problem. He joined his wife at the window and said, "Quit whining. It's not like we are paying for this room out of our own pocket. Besides, haven't you seen a lake before? This way, we won't have the sun shining in our eyes at 5:00 a.m. I'm going to see what's on cable. I presume they have ESPN. Meanwhile, if you're going to hang out on that balcony, could you at least close the door? It's hot out there. You're letting out all the air conditioning."

Carla Sorgren remained on the balcony but closed the sliding glass door and looked at her husband with a mixture of resentment and resignation. He was lying crossways on the bed in a way that insured his feet would soil the bedspread. It was the same rude and negligent manner that he always assumed at home. She could still remember why she married him when she noted that particular habit. I mean, he had been the big basketball star at Saint Cloud State University, a "Fighting Husky." It was cool the way that the other sorority girls gushed when he ducked under the doorways of the house. They had made rude and suggestive comments that Carla fielded with ribald nonchalance—fantasy was always so much better than the real thing. So now here he was, thinner than ever, balding, with bad breath, and perpetually scratching. In the deep recesses of her soul, she knew that she still "loved her man," but he was gradually being stolen from her by a seemingly omnipotent rival. When she had first confronted Alan about his new hobby, he had promised her it was something he could control, he didn't have a habit and he hardly ever used the stuff. "I mean," he said, "if I'm supposed to keep this stuff out of the hands of kids, I'd better know what I'm talking about. Don't be so high and mighty! You could try some, too. A little won't hurt."

Well, maybe it hadn't hurt him, but it hadn't done her any good. To be sure, it had been grand at first, but when she lost her first tooth, she made a decision that she had never regretted. She went off the stuff for good. Alan said he would do the same. It seemed, however, that his ordeal of withdrawal was so much easier than hers had been. And once she was totally off the meth, and feeling good again, it felt so satisfying to eat. She wondered if carrying around forty extra pounds was healthier than using meth. It had to be!

But Alan? He never gained a pound. His nose seemed to run more than it should. Sadly, she knew why. He had lied about quitting the stuff. It made her sad, but she had lately started to realize it was a problem that she had to cope with by herself and that she could do only so much for him. She found a website for families of methamphetamine users and she was determined to stick by him.

In any event, he was certainly right about the heat. It was hot outside and the humidity made her clothes stick to her skin. She went in the room and said, "Well, what did you find?"

"Oh, there's a game between the Pittsburgh Pirates and the Saint Louis Cardinals."

"What could you possibly care about two National League baseball teams? Now, if the Twins were playing, maybe I could understand it. You've never even been to either of those cities."

"C'mon," Alan said. "It's baseball."

"So, are you planning to lay there and watch that stupid game until it is time for the banquet?"

"What else you think I should do? Want me to take you to that K-Mart you were talking about? With any luck we could hit up a blue light special."

"No, I do not," Carla said testily, "but I don't want to sit here either. I saw from the balcony a little gift shop across the street. It's called Paul's Presents. Maybe I'll just walk over there and do a little shopping. Want to come along?"

In truth, Alan had yearned for just a little privacy ever since they had left home. He tried not to sound too eager when he said, "No, that's all right. Why don't you go and take all the time you need. I'll just enjoy the game and be here when you get back."

Carla sighed deeply and said, "Right then. I'll take the key with me in case you fall asleep." She eased out of the room and closed the door.

Alan Sorgren waited until he could see her cross the street before he frantically grabbed his shaving kit. He had just a little present for himself in a non-descript pill bottle. "I'll get by with a little help from my friends," he hummed.

It was always like this. Anticipation, then euphoria, but then, inevitably, regret, and self-recrimination. How had he let this happen to him? As he always did, he became lachry-mose and sought others to blame. *If he hadn't set the whole thing up the first time, if he hadn't forced me to be a part of that whole thing, I wouldn't be this way. Carla pointed out that I didn't have to go along, but she wasn't there at the time. It seemed so innocent. I thought I was doing the right thing. He told me to do it. He said I would love it and be a better sheriff because of it. Well, I sure loved it. And Carla loved it, too, when she tried it. Loved it more than I did, if it came to that.*

I can't help but wonder if he ever takes it himself, he doesn't seem like he does. And now that he has his hooks in me, it's like he sneers at my weakness. God, that first time I told him that I had found a meth lab in my county, run by residents of his county, I thought we could get together and stage a big raid that would make us both famous. Wow, did I learn a lesson. My fellow sheriff, a middle man for a methamphetamine distribution ring, and I couldn't do anything about it because he would let it slip that I had been using a little of the product which he said he had confiscated in an earlier raid. So I kept my mouth shut and have got all I wanted for free ever since. And now, it would seem, someone else knows. But if he knows about me, he also knows about Green.

I suppose that hypocritical sleezeball will be at the banquet tonight, posing as the northern equivalent of Palmer Knutson. Somebody should do something about him. One could hope that some criminal could come back and take revenge on him, but that would assume he ever put a criminal behind bars instead of just taking a cut of the crime himself, Alan told himself, pacing the room, talking to the full length mirror on the wall

Meanwhile, Carla roamed the aisles of the gift store, sadly picking up and examining cedar jewel boxes and deerskin slippers. She had to help Alan, but to do that, she had to get to the source of the problem. The corrupt sheriff. He seemed charming when he delivered those special little packets and winked at them. But now he seemed to be the devil incarnate. She supposed he would be there for the conference. Could she contain herself? To denounce him was out of the question of course, because that would only bring attention to Alan and her. But someone should do something about him, and do it fast.

* *

Ronnie Erstad opened the door of room 428, took a cautious peek in, and said, "Oooh, this is nice. And so cool!" He deposited the wheeled suitcase beside the door and literally dove onto the bed. Erstead never did anything half way. A perpetual optimist who was often totally oblivious to those around him, he lazed back with his hands behind his head and said, "Isn't this nice, dear?"

Denise Erstead, who was still standing in the doorway said, "I guess so. It looks like a hotel room. It's got a television, a bed, a desk, and a window, and I presume a bathroom, so, yeah, I guess it's fine." She closed the door and went to see if it indeed did have a bathroom.

Ronnie looked out the window. "What a great view from up here. Isn't that a nice lake? Wouldn't it be fun to be out on the lake, tearing around in our own boat?"

"Yes, love, I'm sure it would be. It would at least be better than spending any more time at those stupid marine stores you seem to love to drag me to. You've been talking about getting a boat for years. So do it, if you think you have to. You don't need my permission," Denise said modestly.

"But you know I want you to be as happy about getting a boat as I would be. Think how much fun we could have with the boys out on the boat. We could all go fishing, we could learn to water ski, we could even take it to Detroit Lakes on the Fourth of July and watch the fireworks—put 'er right out in the middle of the lake, away from all the mosquitoes. I've always wanted to do that."

"I suppose it's occurred to you that we don't own a lake cottage, and that we are an hour's drive from the nearest decent lake. Or are you thinking of waiting until there's another great flood so you can drive around in the ditches. We must live in the flattest county in the state."

In this rather sour statement, Denise was not far wrong. Harrison County, on the Red River of the North, was in the middle of what was once ancient Lake Agassiz. It was a great place for wheat and sugar beets, but it was hardly the view of Minnesota that was in all the travel literature.

Ronnie had been sheriff for ten years and had no ambitions to do anything else. Who would ever vote against him? There were times when Denise thought she just might. "I'm sorry to be so negative," she now said, "but how would you use a boat if we had one."

"Oh, that would be no problem. We would just have to get a boat trailer—well everybody gets one of them anyway—and we can just park it in the back yard. They always come with those little canvas covers, you know. I mean, if people from our area own a lake cottage, they have to drive to it anyway. We can just drag the boat behind and go to any lake that has public access. That's the beauty of it. We can go to any lake we want to. A different lake every time if we like! That's free! We don't even have to pay extra taxes. All right, we pay for a boat license, but that's it. Besides, you know, you make fun of driving the boat in the ditches, but there are times when a boat is needed, if not in the ditches, then in a flood of the Red River or one of our other rivers. Do you realize that during the great flood of 1997 the Red River was thirty miles wide north of Grand Forks? I should be able to use some county funds to buy the boat, some kind of shared ownership deal. I'm going to talk it over with the county commissioners."

"I don't suppose you have any particular boat in mind?" Denise asked cautiously.

"Of course. It's the one I was just looking at Paul Bunyan Marine?"

"That flashy red one?"

Ronnie almost began to drool. "You bet. That was a Lund 186 Type GL. It's almost a brand new model. It only came out in 2007. Lund makes the best fiberglass boats in the business, you know. Here, look at the literature I picked up. I'm telling you, I think this is the one."

Denise sighed, "If you like it, I'm sure it will be just swell. However, and not to curb your enthusiasm, what happens if the county won't kick in any money? Can we afford it by ourselves."

"I don't know. Maybe. As long as 'you-know-who' doesn't gum things up for us. I mean, here's a guy, sheriff of a small county himself, who comes up with a plan to share the office of sheriff with other counties. Of course, his idea was that he could handle the duties of two counties all by himself. Well, that would have required action down in St. Paul, and it didn't fly last year, but it was close. If he can pull off that stunt, and absorb the sheriff's office of another county, what would be the future of my job? We are surrounded by bigger, richer counties, and our county has fewer people than the one he wants to gobble up. What would I do then? No boat, I'll tell you."

"Is anybody else pushing that agenda?"

"Maybe. There's this other sheriff, a young guy who seems to have ambitions, who's making sounds like he could handle two counties. I'm going to have to have a little one-on-one with him during the conference. But old Green is the one behind it, I'm sure."

Can anybody stop him?"

"That weasel? Well, somebody has to. Maybe we should do something about him."

* *

Kevin Charbonneau was proud of his heritage. His great grandfather had been part of Louis Riel's rebellion in southern Manitoba that challenged the governments of both Canada and the United States. He was part Metis—a mixture of Native American Cree and French. His ancestors had been in Northwestern Minnesota before statehood and had loaded their ox carts with hides and furs and had driven them five hundred miles down to St. Paul. He could still find the deep tracks that passed through his county and every time he saw them he reflected about how his ancestors would have been amazed that one of their own was sheriff of Carson County.

Coming to Bemidji was like coming home for Charbonneau. He had graduated from Bemidji State University only five years earlier. College life was good life. He had a job with campus security and was a member of the mile relay team of the Beaver's track and field squad. He never minded when team members or the opposition called him Frenchy or MonSewer, but woe to him who made fun of his Indian heritage. He was darkly handsome, quick witted, and popular. No wonder Jenny had fallen for him.

"Have you ever been here before?" Jenny asked, as she put the key into the lock of room 356.

"I've been in the building, sure. A couple of wedding receptions and a sports banquet. But I've never stayed here. College kids would never stay in a Radisson. We were lucky to afford ten people to a room at the Super 8."

Jenny had married Kevin only two years earlier. Perhaps one might call her pleasant looking rather than beautiful, with short brown hair, brown eyes that danced for everyone, and a rather large nose with inordinately large nostrils. She accepted this unusual feature with aplomb and would often say she could "smell a bargain, a rat, a phony, or something fishy" better than anyone in the world. "Well," she now said, "it is certainly better than any room I've ever stayed in. I mean, our honeymoon cabin on the North Shore was nice, but look at that bed. This is elegant. I wish I could stay."

"I wish you could, too. It would be free. I mean, it's the same price for the room whether you're here or not. Are you sure you won't change your mind?"

"No, Sandra's been looking forward to this. She's been after me to come to her place in Duluth for a long time. I haven't seen her since last summer and I do like to spend time with my nieces and my nephew. She says I spoil them rotten every time we get together, but what's an aunt for? Besides, I can stay with them and provide free babysitting while she and Bart go out on the town."

"So, there's an 'out on the town' lifestyle in Duluth?"

"Well, you know. It doesn't matter so much what you do, it is just nice to get away from the kids for a few hours. So I'm told, anyway. Speaking of which, er, um, have you given any more thought to what we talked about last weekend?"

"Starting a family, you mean? Yeah, I guess that would be all right. I should get a raise next year. I don't want the family name to die out, after all."

"So, you want a boy, do you?"

"All right then, the family line. That better? How long will it take you to get to Duluth?"

"If I don't get stopped by the fuzz, I should make it in a little over two hours. It's just straight down Highway 2. I told her I would be there for supper."

"I suppose you better get going then, so you don't have to speed and I have to live with the shame of 'Sheriff's wife flouts law!' Give me a kiss.

Following a long passionate kiss, Jenny left and Kevin flopped down on the bed, turned on the TV, and scrolled through the channels. Sudden departures like that always made him immediately lonesome.

"Nevertheless," he mused, "this could be an interesting conference. And for what I have planned, I definitely do not need Jenny around."

Sheriff Kevin Charbonneau, the youngest elected sheriff in Minnesota, was a collector. Not of baseball cards, or coins, or Hummel figurines, but of information. He kept a thick file in his office of all that he had heard, substantiated or not, of possible villains, heroes, and fools, not the least of which, depending on the category, included information on his fellow law enforcement officers. In the three years since he had been elected, the file had grown enormously. But the file was just for reference, he rarely consulted it, because he had a fabulous memory for facts and faces. Not that he ever intended to use most of the information, at least, never in an unethical way. But ethics tend to vary with the person who forms them, and Charbonneau's were a unique blend of utilitarianism, opportunism, and a conviction that ultimate truth did exist, and that he was the best to determine the nature of that truth.

He had been like that as long as he could remember. He always had a mission in life, and it was to further the cause of justice. There was nothing that offended his sense of justice more than a betrayal of the law by those sworn to uphold it. As a college student, he had taken a course in the history of the French Revolution. He was drawn to Robespierre—Robespierre the Incorruptible—and expounded his values one night during a dormitory bull session. One of his friends said, "You know why you admire him, don't you? It's because you are just like him. We should call you 'Kevin the Incorruptible.'" Charbonneau did the expected amount of ridiculing the notion, but inwardly he gloried in the appellation.

So, he thought, *tonight I will see how many of my colleagues are still engaged in their somewhat unprofessional practices. It should be fun to drop a tiny little hint that I know what they are up to. Or, better yet, just mention something innocently that barely touches on the topic. That way, they can go away and wonder, "What does he know?" Therefore, if they suddenly see the need to confide in me, I can act totally surprised and profess to be overly supportive. All of those old fools have been feeding at the public trough for so long that they will do anything to avoid anything unpleasant. It should be fun to see their faces as they kick themselves for confiding in me when I tell them it was all a shock to me. Spilled their guts for nothing! Ha! Thank God there are some decent members of the profession. Most of the new breed, and some of the old, like Palmer Knutson, are what law enforcement is all about. Why should we have to settle for less?*

Of course, there is the special bit of news that I am saving for one very special person. The old motto that revenge is a dish best served cold will be tested tonight. Ah, my diner of chilly food, you will freeze your filthy belly!

❖ ❖

Harvey Green wheezed as he tossed his small suitcase on the desk of room 342. It may have been small, but it was heavy. Green wasted no time grabbing the ice bucket and going back out the door. He came back with a full bucket of ice, only to find that he couldn't open his door. Painfully he remembered setting the card down on the desk when he picked up the ice bucket. He swore so loudly and viciously that a maid, at the extreme end of the hall, came out of a room to attend to an emergency, grabbing her cell phone in case it might be necessary to call 911. She looked up as Green gave the door a ferocious kick and turned the air around him a profane blue. She rushed up and asked, "Is there some trouble, sir?"

This polite inquiry was followed by another stream of invective, from which the maid was able to determine that the guest had merely locked himself out of his room. Without saying a word, she opened the door and abruptly turned away. Gratitude was not a strong suit of Harvey, but her brusqueness so shocked him that he muttered a barely audible 'thanks' to her retreating figure.

Back in his room, the reason for the heft of the suitcase was soon revealed. From out of it, Green took a 1.75 liter bottle of Canadian Club and a liter of club soda. He poured a generous slug, turned on the TV, sat down, and broke wind.

His thoughts turned to the upcoming conference. He regretted that it was no longer held at the good old Grundorf Pines Resort. He always got a nice kickback from brother Harley for that, and besides, it was always so easy to control things there. If a guy wanted to fish a little early, well, what the hell, give him a boat and let him fish. Of course, that meant that if he needed a little favor from that neighboring sheriff, all he needed to do was to mention his hospitality. The booze and the girls, well, discretion should never be cheap.

But this traveling conference ended all that. More disturbing, however, was the news that somebody was looking into things that did not concern him. He did not know who, but he assumed it involved the possessor of one of the multitude of the toes that he had stepped on. Well, he could always find some way to turn the screws. *Everybody has a price,* he figured, *except maybe that goodie-goodie-two-shoes Palmer Knutson and his ilk. Even he's an all-right sort—he's never taken anything from me, so he don't owe me. No, whoever is doing the digging now is a nastier sort. And if he's looking into what he seems to be looking into, well, that has to stop. I wonder what his price will be.*

Green was glad to be back into what he considered to be civilization. He always said, tiresomely, that Grundorf was not the end of the world but that one could see it from there. Lately, he had been spending a little more time in Winnipeg than anywhere else. He had a special friend there. To be sure, he had to come up with some excuse for his wife as to how it could be official business to spend time in Canada, but he had come up with a beautiful scenario in which some scheme existed to sell Canadian prescription drugs under the counter to shady pharmacists in the United States. Since this was "government stuff" he couldn't really tell her much about it, "you understand," but when it was all over he would be free to talk all about it.

So every other weekend he would cross the border and drive to Winnipeg, meet his special friend, and spend the weekend in their own special love nest. They would delight in going to the Red Lantern Restaurant in the French section of town called St. Boniface. They would go to the Assinaboin Zoo, or even take in a special event. One weekend they even went to the opera. Hoo-boy, if the other sheriffs at this conference could have seen that! Of course, it was understood that his wife would never accompany him to the sheriff's conference. But now that he thought about it, his relationship with his special friend in Winnipeg had liberated the old constraints. Maybe he could even do a little flirting at the conference. Of course, he would never tell his special friend, Dave, about that!

CHAPTER FOUR

I T WAS TIME FOR THE NBC NIGHTLY NEWS with Brian Williams. Ellie was a recent convert to NBC. She had watched the master, Saint Peter Jennings, for years, but he was gone and she had tried to keep allegiance to ABC. As she saw it, however, that network had failed her. Brian Williams may not have been Peter Jennings, but at least he could be humorous and occasionally poetic. Palmer generally agreed, but did not enjoy the national news. Part of it was that Ellie always saw the need to talk back to the talking heads. If the prime minister of Israel denounced the Palestinians, Ellie would argue with him, and if someone said a kind word about George W. Bush, she would slander him. It was, considered Palmer Knutson, "ineffective communication."

"You know," he said, "I think I'll just go down to the lobby to see who has checked in for the conference. There might be someone around to chew the fat with. I presume you won't miss me as long as you have your friend Brian to keep you company."

Ellie's reply was, "Yeah, right! And how much did the oil companies give your campaign last time?" Palmer was briefly bewildered as to why an oil company would contribute to the election campaign of a county sheriff, until he realized that the unwitting target of the question was on the television screen. He quietly let himself out of the room and took the elevator down to the lobby.

There is a depressing sameness to hotel elevators, and yet, that sameness allows one uninterrupted reverie. Palmer could still remember the first time he had been in an elevator. His father had some business to do in Fargo and he had taken Palmer to the "Top of the Mart," a bar at the top of the Frederick Martin Hotel in Moorhead. He made Palmer promise not to tell his mom that he had taken him into a bar, but told Palmer he would never forget the view from the top of the eighth floor hotel. Apparently, he had been right.

When the elevator doors opened on the main floor, Palmer could see that the lobby was starting to fill up with sheriffs and deputies, some of whom he looked forward to talking with and some to be avoided. The line in front of the registration table was the longest he had ever seen for the conference. There were sheriffs wearing navy-blue sport coats with wing tip shoes and there were sheriffs in Hawaiian shirts with white shoes and white belts. There were unidentifiable deputies, wives, and girlfriends of all sizes and ages. As he walked to the middle of the room, and was subject to various good-humored bellows of "Hey, Palmer," he was deftly intercepted by Jason Two Bears. For some reason Two Bears seemed anxious to get Palmer out of the room. He said, "Palmer! I've been keeping an eye out for you. Let me take you into the bar where we can find a quiet corner and I'll buy you a beer."

Since Palmer liked the young deputy and wanted to know more about his old friend Sheriff Meyer, it was an offer he could not refuse. A short beer in a tall glass seemed like an excellent idea.

Jason guided Palmer to a quiet corner of the bar and said, "How about a Beck's?"

It was music to Palmer's ears. As they sat in mutual appreciation of the situation, waiting for the beer to arrive, Palmer was struck by the uncompromising nature of Two Bear's face. He possessed every characteristic associated with Native Americans, from his high cheekbones, to his deep-brown eyes and thick black hair. He was of only average height, but he carried himself with an attitude that virtually proclaimed pride and confidence. The first time Palmer met him he was somewhat unnerved by the thought that here was a face that expressed absolutely no emotion. And then Two Bears smiled. Palmer saw joy, wit, and intelligence. Jason was smiling now as the beer was placed on the table. Only then did Palmer say, "I was so shocked to hear about Neal. Is it serious?"

Jason Two Bears smiled and said, "No, it isn't serious." It seems that when he went in for a physical checkup, they found a suspicious little spot on his forehead. Now, you know Neal, he was never happier than when he was out in his boat with his line in the water. Sometimes he even bothered to bait the hook. Well, all that time, he never put on any sunscreen or even wore a hat and as a result he had a little patch of skin cancer. They were able to remove it right in the doctor's office and he walked around with a band-aid on his head for a couple of days. But, you know, there's hardly a word in the English language more scary than 'cancer.' Neal went home, talked to his wife, and the next day he handed in his resignation. Even as we speak, he is up in northern Saskatchewan floating on Lake Athabasca pulling in walleyes the size of elephant seals. He just left two days ago, but before he did, he said he had two regrets to pass on to you. The first regret was that he hadn't quit sooner, and the second regret was that he wouldn't get a chance to see you tonight. I'm not buying this beer just because I like you, which I do anyway, but because I received strict orders to do so."

Palmer smiled, took a long pull on his beer, and said, "So, that means you're in charge then."

"Yep."

"For how long?"

"Don't know. I don't think anybody does. I mean, the county board had no choice but to accept his resignation— Neal made it clear he was gone in any event—but they haven't done anything about it. Neal appointed me to be next in line, so I am the 'acting' sheriff. If they want to change things, I suppose they could, but I presume they'll just wait for the next election, which won't be for another year and a half. Of course, they could call a special election, and there are some in the county who'd like to see that happen."

"How come?"

Two Bears scowled. "Why do you suppose? Do you think this county is totally filled with tolerant people? Maybe it isn't any more prejudiced than any other county, but it isn't any less either. Some think having an Indian sheriff would be quaint, you know, the chamber of commerce types who think I could be sort of a Northern Minnesota Tony Hillerman creation. Instead of roaming around Arizona or New Mexico, I'll be the one who can wander around the woods using my native cunning to solve crime. Sure, there are those who might be very proud that their region had at last surmounted discrimination and had a Native American sheriff. Most people, I suppose, might think it is just the way the world changes, not necessarily for the better, but who are willing to live with it. Unfortunately, there are those with deep-set prejudice who will never accept an 'Injun' for their sheriff. I mean, look at all those old westerns. A guy got to be sheriff by killing Indians."

This kind of talk made Palmer uncomfortable. "Have you seen much of that, er, you know?"

Two Bears sighed and said, "No, not too much. Ever since I was made acting sheriff, there have been a few times when I have been called 'chief.' I never felt it was meant in a mean way and I've known most of those people for a long time anyway. It was kind of funny yesterday when Milt

Johnson, our youngest deputy, responded to an order with a 'yes, Chief.' Well, that was what he used to say to Neal. So he said that and immediately turned red to the roots of his yellow hair. He started to mumble something incoherent and I just said, "That's all right, you can call me 'Chief.' Unfortunately, the nastiest comments have actually come from another member of the profession."

"What? Who?"

Two Bears stopped fiddling with his beer napkin, looked Palmer in the eye, and said, "Now who would you guess? Harvey Green, perhaps?"

"Yah, I suppose I would. What did he say?" Palmer asked with nervous trepidation.

"Oh, the usual, for someone of his level of sophistication. 'Now that you chief, you gettum more wompom and add new addition to teepee?' 'You gonna catch crooks red handed?' Actually, I had to kind of laugh later at that one. But you know, we have an Anishinaabe word for someone like him. It is pronounced ahs-ho-el."

Palmer giggled. "You know, there's an English equivalent word, and it is pronounced the very same way. An excellent word for him! Well, the trip hasn't been a total waste of time, now that I have learned some sophisticated Native American language. Why do you suppose he's such an ignorant bigot?"

"Don't you know?" Two Bears put up two fingers for two more Beck's. "First of all, he comes by it naturally. Look at his family! Then, of course, he isn't very smart. Never did finish college. But more than anything, it goes back to *Bryan v. Itasca County.*"

"Say what?"

"Not heard of it? Few people have. It goes back to 1972 when a member of my tribe, Russell Bryan, received a tax bill from Itasca County for $147.95. This was on a mobile home that he owned on the Leech Lake Reservation, and he refused to pay it, claiming that state tax laws didn't apply to an Indian living on a reservation. The case went all the way to the U.S. Supreme Court where it was a unanimous decision in favor of Bryan. Basically, this became the legal cornerstone for the principle that the states cannot regulate the activities of Indians on reservations without explicit authority from Congress. You see where this is going?"

"I think I do, yes. To reservation casinos."

"Exactly. And now there are casinos in Thief River Falls, Mahnomen, Duluth, Hinkley, and several other places. And it's all over the country! Now can you see why Harvey Green doesn't particularly like Indians?"

"I see," Palmer said, "You're telling me that they took over big time from the small-time illegal gambling operations that went on in his family's resort."

"Bingo, as we say in our casinos."

Palmer smiled, "Is there another good Ojibwe word that you can teach me to describe him?"

"There might be, but I think we have already found the perfect word."

"Yes, I think we have. By the way, there was something I was going to ask you. I think you would be too young to remember this, but do you know anything about a guy who claimed to be an Indian chief who would sell souvenirs and pose for pictures in Itasca Park. This was, I suppose, in the fifties?"

"Somebody else asked me that not too long ago, and the short answer is, no. I did ask around, though, and I got a lot of conflicting answers. One guy claimed it was his uncle, another claimed that the guy really was a chief, but not from around here. I talked to an old man at the nursing home in Bemidji who claimed that he was an Indian all right, but not Ojibwe. He said he was Sioux. Now, we consider the Sioux our brothers, of course, but that doesn't mean we always see eye to eye with them. Those are the guys who let the University of North Dakota use them as human mascots for all those years. "UND—Home of the Fighting Sioux." It's one of the main reasons why I went to North Dakota State. Go Bison!"

"I was going to ask you about that. How's that going?"

Jason leaned forward and said, "Can you keep a secret?"

Palmer said, "For someone who buys me beer, I am the soul of discretion. What's up?"

"I'm glad I got appointed to acting sheriff, but I don't intend to keep doing this. As you know, I've been taking courses in criminal justice at NDSU for a long time. After I got my Master's Degree, I was still in the habit of going there in the summer and during weekends, I enjoyed it and I just kept at it. I can get a teaching assistantship that will enable me to get my PhD in two years. I feel a little guilty about it, because not only did Neal stick his neck out for me, but in the last week I have been greatly honored by members of my own tribe. But a man gotta do what a man gotta do. I'll give it until the next election, and then decline to run."

Palmer, said, "So you would rather be a professor than a sheriff?"

"Wouldn't you?"

Palmer had often asked himself this same question. He had gone into law enforcement for the time being, a period that had extended almost forty years. He lugubriously nodded and said, "I think sometimes maybe I would. But why?"

"It's not the idea of the profession, the working conditions, the pay, or anything like that. I still think that what I do does make a difference. But I'm sick of the unevenness of the whole thing, if there is a word like that. I see dedicated people like you and like a few members of the Bemidji Police Force, which is very good, by the way, and I'm proud to be a part of the whole profession. But then there are people like

Harvey Green, and several more people attending this conference who are just good old boys who regret that there are no longer hippies to beat up. You work hard and have an excellent staff, like Neal put together, and then you go down to the cities and they treat you like you're Barney Fife of Mayberry RFD. Something happens on the reservation and ignorant feds come out and tell you what to do and you just know that it is the wrong thing to do but you don't have much choice. After a while, you just want to say 'to hell with it.' And that is exactly what I'm going to do."

Palmer grinned and raised his glass. "Good for you. I like the sound of it. Dr. Two Bears. But you know, I 'spose I should get ready for the banquet. I gotta give that speech and I imagine Ellie is wondering where I've wandered off to. Since you represent the home county, will you be serving as the emcee tonight?"

"Yep."

"So you're going to announce me?"

"Well, sort of, everybody already knows who you are."

"Do you need any additional information?"

"Let's see, the title of your address is 'The Value of Tax-Funded Law Enforcement at the County Level for the Twenty-First Century.' That right?"

"Yah."

"Catchy! Other than that, I think I know enough about you. I'll see you in about, um, half an hour?"

Palmer went out of the bar and walked by the reservations desk. He noticed the bowl of bright red apples and out of habit took one. It wasn't that he intended to eat it, at least, not in the near future, but at the price he had to pay for his room, he decided the county should get its money's worth.

CHAPTER FIVE

A S PALMER OPENED THE DOOR TO THEIR ROOM he heard Ellie say, "Oh, come on! You lie! Your feet stink! And you don't love the Lord Jesus!"

Palmer assumed, correctly, that she was not addressing him. "Congressman Paulson on television again, dear?"

"Yeah. He just got done trying to answer a reporter who asked him how he could pontificate about 'right to life' in one breath while supporting capital punishment with the other. He tried to change the subject and basically ended up saying that if everybody was armed with handguns the whole problem would disappear. At least, that's what it sounded like. He is so oily! I'd like to see him try to pick up an olive with his bare fingers! So, you must have found somebody to talk to."

"Ya, I've been talking to Jason Two Bears. He's a swell guy. He's running the show tonight, you know, since Neal Meyer took off for Canada. But I thought maybe I should get dressed and go through my speech one more time. Have you had a chance to read it since I added a couple of jokes?"

"Um, yes. Are you sure you want to use them all. They sort of remind me of the jokes written in our *Weekly Reader* in fifth grade. This will be a room full of adults, you know. I mean, everybody knows where Napoleon kept his big armies at the Battle of Waterloo, but do you know where he kept his little armies? Up his little sleevies! Har Har. First of all, many of the people in that room will not have the slightest notion as to who Napoleon was, let alone what happened at Waterloo. Little sleevies!"

"Well, you know, I thought I should avoid anything that could be considered blue, political, ethnic or sexist humor. That's not as easy as it would seem."

Ellie raised her eyebrows and shook her head and said, "Well, see how it goes. It's been my experience that the audience will laugh at anything if they like the speaker, and will growl at the funniest joke if they hate him. I think that crowd will forgive you a multitude of sins."

"Um, kind of you to say so," Palmer said semi-sarcastically.

Palmer took his manuscript into the bathroom so Ellie could watch yet another re-run of Seinfeld. Knutson was not a bad speaker, but always preferred to speak from a full manuscript. He was making some technical points concerning taxation and wise expenditures, but he wanted to make sure he had everything down. He even had his jokes annotated as to where he should pause for the best effect.

At last Palmer considered himself ready. He came back into the room and began to change into his fine suit. When he finished tying his shoes, he noticed Ellie out on the balcony. Hitching his pants up slightly higher than normal, to help him contain what he considered to be an unsightly bulge, he joined her.

"Woo, it sure is humid out here. Think it will storm?"

Ellie nodded. "The weatherman on the six o'clock news said that we were under a tornado watch. It's so still. It's almost creepy. Look how that high gray cloud has perfectly marked the leading edge of the cold front. Oh, yeah, it will storm all right. And not too long from now."

At five minutes to seven they made their way down to the ballroom for the banquet. At the door, he was shocked to see Orly Peterson and his new bride, Allysha.

"Orly! Allysha! What are you doing here?"

"Well, that doesn't make us feel too welcome. Why shouldn't we be here?" Orly snarled.

"No, no, I didn't mean that. We're glad to see you, and all that, but I thought you took the weekend off so you could go to some resort."

"That's true, but not to a resort. Allysha's family is having a reunion at her uncle's cabin on Lake Plantagenet. We thought it would be nice to be here and show a little support for you from good old Otter Tail County, that's all."

Palmer was touched. It had now been several years that he and Orly had been working together. He had hired him, ("against my better judgment," he had informed Ellie) fresh out of the criminal justice department at Fergus Falls State University. His grades and recommendations were exemplary, and Palmer eventually realized that the main reason he hesitated in hiring him was that he was "such a Swede." Orly also made him tired. He was a rather enthusiastic servant of the people, not that there was anything wrong with that, of course, but it irked Palmer to see him always in a pressed uniform with his L.A.P.D. sunglasses. He was sure that Orly only assumed the appearance because it attracted women. Nevertheless, ever since Palmer had appointed him as his chief deputy, they had gradually become friends.

"So," Orly continued, "got your speech all ready? If so, the cash bar is still open. How about if I get you a beer? I know, I know, I won't get Budweiser, since it tastes like it has been passed through a Clydesdale. And they don't have that Norwegian Ringnes. How 'bout a Heiniken?"

"Well, I should probably stay sober for my speech, but on the other hand, maybe it will be better if I'm not. Okay, since you're buying, why not?"

Orly turned to Ellie and said, "And how about you?"

"I guess I'll have what he's having. Thank you, Orly."

"Com'on, Allysha, you can help me carry the beer."

As Orly and Allysha headed to the bar, Palmer noticed most of the masculine eyes in the room following the new bride's movement. To Ellie, he said, "Isn't that nice. I hope they reserved a place well in advance. I've never seen this meeting attended this well. It kinda makes me nervous."

For twenty minutes people milled around, coming to talk to Palmer and Ellie, exchanging pleasantries and enquiring about respective families and acquaintances. Eventually, Jason Two Bears stood at the head table and banged a spoon on a water glass to order people to their tables. When the conference had first started, old Pastor Vernquist, a sheriff-become minister, offered a blessing on the meal. Since he had joined the heavenly choir, however, no one had replaced him. People began to eat the bread roll and await the entrée. Palmer was surprised to note that while Two Bears was on his left, as was only proper, Orly and Allysha, were also seated at the head table immediately to his right. How come Orly deserved such treatment? Palmer discussed the weather with Two Bears while Ellie discussed the weather with Orly.

At last, as the coffee was being poured and the skimpy carrot cake was being brought out by the high school kids hired to serve the banquet, Two Bears stood up and said, "On behalf of Beltrami County and the City of Bemidji, I'd like to welcome you to the Twenty-fifth meeting of the Northwestern Minnesota Association of County Sheriffs. When it came our turn to host the conference, Sheriff Meyer and I met with the two previous hosts so that they could help us plan. By the way, as I'm sure many of you know, Neil resigned last week and is currently trying to outwit the fish in northern Canada. Meanwhile, I'm now the acting sheriff in this county, so if any of you people out there get in trouble during this conference, it won't do you any good to have known Neil Meyer for twenty years." A small chuckle emerged from the audience, many of whom did not know the extent of his seriousness. As if sensing the unease, Two

Bears continued, "Seriously, though, I was with Neil when we started planning this conference. There had been a small amount of funds left over from the last two conferences, and someone suggested that we ought to start a new tradition of awarding recognition to an individual who had significantly contributed to our profession. This was easily decided, and the next question, 'Who should be our first honoree?' was even easier to agree upon. To introduce the first recipient of this award, I will now call upon Orly Peterson of Otter Tail County. Orly?"

As Orly straightened his handsome six-foot frame before the podium he looked back at Palmer. For the first time, Palmer began to put everything together. There was that special effort to make sure Ellie came along. There was the size of the crowd, the smirky expectant look on so many of the faces he had seen all day, and, of course, the presence of Orly Peterson at the head table. He thought, "Open the Gates of the Temple! I'm about to be honored!"

Orly began, "Ladies and Gentlemen, for the last five years it has been my privilege to have worked with one of the finest law enforcement officers in the state of Minnesota. I give you, Palmer Knutson."

Thunderous applause rang out, as some people literally leapt to their feet and cheered. Others, with perhaps less enthusiasm for Knutson, or at least some greater respect for the tradition of a standing ovation, took longer to stand, not wanting to create the impression that they were disapproving of the award. Palmer, with a countenance the shade of sun-dried tomato soup, stood and nodded and muttered "thank yous." At last, the multitude sat and Peterson continued. "The position of sheriff in Minnesota, as you are all aware, is an elected one. This means that the sheriff must, at regular intervals, submit to the approval of the people he is elected to serve. Ladies and gentlemen, since becoming the sheriff of Otter Tail County, Sheriff Knutson's margin of electoral victory has increased every time. In fact, he has been unopposed for as long as I can remember," Peterson took a calm breath and continued.

"County sheriffs provide the face of law and order for the people. Village constables, city police, and the highway patrol all have vital and respected roles in law enforcement, but it is the county sheriff who handles the widest variety of tasks affecting the people. They serve tax judgments, handle domestic disputes, examine traffic accidents, and do literally hundreds of other tasks most people have never considered. In rare times, the county sheriff is called upon to perform extraordinary duties. In the time I have been at the side of Sheriff Knutson, he has solved three high profile murder cases, a performance that has gained him statewide, even national, recognition." The audience gave a short applause.

"Furthermore, you must remember that he has done all this in spite of the fact that he's a Norwegian."

"*Oh, God, here it comes,*" thought Palmer, but for once without the usual resentment.

"Palmer's relatives have always been hardworking, and one time his Uncle Ole decided that he was going to clear about an acre of brush on some lake property that he owned. So he goes to the hardware store and tells the guy that he wants a saw that could cut down about a hundred small trees in a day. The guy at the hardware store says, 'I got just the saw for you.' Well Ole, he buys the saw and goes out to work. But he comes back to the hardware store the next evening and says, 'Dis here ting doesn't verk?' 'What do you mean, it doesn't work,' says the hardware man. 'Vell,' Ole says, 'I took dis ting out to da woods today and I verked and verked and I only got von tree cut down.'

'Hmmm,' says that hardware guy. He starts fiddling with all the knobs and can find nothing wrong with it, so he gives the starting rope a pull. The saw immediately starts up and Ole says, 'Hey! Vat's dat noise?'"

Fortunately, for Orly, there were still a few who had not heard that joke, and in any event, as Ellie thought, it bore out her contention that people will want to laugh if they like the joke teller. But Orly decided to press his luck.

"Ole is in many ways just like Palmer," added Orly, as he attempted a deft segue. "Palmer likes his lutefisk too. For Ole, though, it was almost like a religion. One day he came into a store and said, 'I vant to buy some lutefisk.' The store owner said, 'I'm sorry we don't have any lutefisk.' Ole was outraged, 'No lutefisk? It's almost tree months until Christmas and yew still don't have lutefisk?' Well, the store owner says, 'You must be Norwegian.' This only made Ole mad. 'Vhy must I be Norvegian? Yust because I ask for lutefisk? If a guy came in here and asked for fish and chips, vould yew assume he vas English? Or if a guy asked for sauerkraut, vould he automatically be Cherman? I s'pose if he asked for a taco yew vould tink he vas Mexican? So yust because I ask for lutefisk yew assume dat I'm Norvegian!!!' The store owner says, 'No, sir, that's not it. You see, this is a hardware store.'"

It seemed fewer people had heard that joke and the response was overwhelming. Orly was temped to go on, but his favorite Ole joke involved Lena and was slightly off-color, so he decided to quit while he was ahead. Besides, he wasn't sure how Palmer was taking this. He needn't have worried, for out of the corner of his eye he saw his boss smiling warmly.

As the laughter died down, Orly said, "Now you may wonder how I know Sheriff Knutson so well. The answer to that, of course, is that I am a Swede. And only a Swede can really know a Norwegian. Therefore, I know Palmer Knutson as the best sheriff in Minnesota. I know that he is a sensitive individual who cares deeply about the people he serves. I have known him to agonize over how to handle a situation wherein a person may be guilty, but may not deserve the full punishment of the law. I have seen him take into consideration all those factors that do not come into the handbook for law enforcement, factors such as age, economic privation, mental and social disabilities, and simple bad luck. I have seen the respect accorded for him by people from all sides of the political spectrum, from immigrants and migrant workers, to his fellow professionals in Saint Paul. It is for this reason, that from this time on, the annual award for the 'Law Enforcement Person of the Year' will be known as the 'Palmer Knutson Award of Distinction.' Ladies and gentlemen, I present to you Palmer Knutson!"

As the ovation rolled across the floor, Palmer leaned over to Ellie and asked, "How long have you known about this?"

She answered, "Oh, for about six months now. Did I do a good job in keeping it a secret?"

"Yes, I'd say you did," said Palmer, as he rose to acknowledge the ovation.

Palmer stepped over to where a grinning Kevin Two Bears was holding an oak-and-brass plaque with Palmer's name engraved on it. He shook hands with Two Bears, Orly, Allysha, and kissed Ellie as he made his way to the podium. He made the universal "settle down" gesture with his hands and waited for the inevitable calm. At last he said, "Well, this is a surprise. Ellie just informed me that she's known about this for six months. Who says spouses can't keep secrets from each other! And Orly, well, I've thought you have been acting a little funny around the office lately, but, in case the rest of you don't know it, Orly is a newly-wed. I thought it was just another case of a nervous groom." A few well-intentioned chuckles passed around the room. "I appreciate your kind words, Orly, especially coming from a Swede. You know, I wasn't sure I wanted a Swede in my office, and the first day I hired Orly I really wondered if I had done the right thing. I mean, here's this gung-ho guy, but he's right out of college and I wanted him to feel at ease in the office. I noticed some candy in the dish at the reception area and I told Orly to go ahead and eat some M and Ms. Next thing you know I see him take a piece of candy and eat it and then take another and throw it in the waste basket. I watched this for a while until I couldn't stand it anymore and asked him what he was doing. He tells me, 'You said I could eat the M and Ms, but half of these are Ws.'" Palmer waited through the chuckles and added, with perfect timing, "Trouble was, like all Swedes, he felt he had to peel each one before he could eat it." More chuckles, as Orly adopted a good-sport-hail-fellow-well-met demeanor.

"But I came to talk to you tonight," Palmer continued, "about something of real importance, the value of tax-funded law enforcement at the county level,"

"Oh, my God," thought Ellie, "does he still intend to give that speech?"

"Taxes are one of the oldest social institutions known to man. We have all heard that old expression that there are only two certainties in life, death and taxes. Taxes are universally despised but accepted. Nevertheless, one may make a case for saying that equitable taxation is the real hallmark of civilization. All of us in law enforcement, from the part time constable, to the highway patrolman, to the big city police commissioner, like Commissioner Gordon of Gotham City, are paid because the citizens have consented to be taxed for their protection." Palmer had hoped to get at least a smile from the Batman reference, but he noticed that eyes were already becoming glazed over.

"The great rallying cry of 1775 was 'No Taxation Without Representation,' a principle that was possibly hinted at in *Magna Carta* but was certainly found in the English Bill of

Rights of 1689. The county commissioners, as you know, set county tax levels, and the state and federal governments provide various and sundry grants to help out. But in each case, these monies are from the citizens and they are technically our bosses. It is our duty, then, to give them the most value for their investment."

Palmer paused. He thought he had come up with a snappy introduction and a penetrating historical analysis. And yet, he noticed the audience fidgeting and checking their watches. He briefly wondered if he should move up some of the jokes. Then it finally dawned on him. The whole speech had been a ruse to get him to the head table and that people were really not expecting him to give a speech. He looked dolefully at the remaining fifteen pages of his manuscript. He was rather proud of it, and it was a shame that it will go to waste.

As these thoughts rapidly flitted though his brain, the hotel desk clerk rapidly came forward for a hurried conversation with Jason Two Bears. The Beltrami County acting sheriff nodded and quickly came to the podium. "Excuse me, Palmer, but I have a rather urgent announcement to make. A tornado warning has just been issued for the city of Bemidji. This is a warning, not just a watch. A funnel cloud has been sighted just fifteen miles southwest of the city moving in our direction. Those of you who do not have rooms at the hotel may wish to leave immediately. Um, Palmer? Perhaps we can arrange to have your remarks printed somewhere. That okay?"

Palmer felt as though he had been saved. The thought, "It's an ill wind that blows nobody good" passed through his mind. In the ballroom, there was nothing but the noise of squeaking chairs and farewell greetings.

Chapter Six

Within five minutes, the ballroom at the Radisson had been cleared except for ten people who decided to wait out the storm in unhurried comfort. Orly had rushed up to Palmer, given him a quick handshake, and panted that if they left immediately they might have a chance to skirt the storm and make it back to Lake Plantagenet. Others either nodded to Palmer in acknowledgment or provided a quick handshake with the assurance that they would see him the next day. The kitchen staff, fully in evidence while Knutson was speaking, seemed to have disappeared. The serving area still had food, plates, serving dishes, and carving pieces sitting in forlorn abandonment. Everyone, it seemed, was intent on battening down the hatches for the oncoming storm. Everyone, that is, except the sheriff of Otter Tail County.

Palmer Knutson loved summer thunderstorms. He remembered being ten years old and standing out in the driveway of his farmhouse with his father as the fierce prairie squall lines advanced upon them. He remembered not being afraid, even as the wind began to howl, as long as he held his dad's hand. Somehow, being comforted by his father's simple theology, he could stand before the tempest and be awed by the force of nature. Fifty years later, he could still feel the wonderment.

The western end of the of the Radisson ballroom featured beautiful floor to ceiling windows. As Knutson pulled the drapes wide, he said to the remaining banqueters, "I think this is probably as safe a place as we can find. We're on the ground floor and we can take more shelter if we need to, but meanwhile we can watch the clouds from here. Would you look at that!"

Everyone immediately saw his point. All but Alan and Carla Sorgren had rooms that faced east, which meant that they could not watch the storm from their rooms, and this was indeed a sight to behold. Heavy low mammary clouds, steel blue with a hint of green, spread across the sky. To the southwest, a wall cloud, almost black, but with wisps of pure white, moved inexorably toward Bemidji. They could see flashes of lightning, but inside the hotel, with the air conditioner humming, they could not yet hear the thunder. Palmer looked around and saw that the staff had left several opened bottles of wine on the open bar counter. He grabbed four bottles and brought them back to the small gathering. With a certain amount of satisfaction he said, "We might as well enjoy ourselves."

This observation met with universal agreement. Wine glasses were filled and soon people began to share stories of earlier storms. Ronnie Erstead said, "In Harrison County, you know, it is so flat that you can stand anywhere and see for miles. I remember, a couple of years ago, we were standing outside watching a storm come in, and it produced this perfect funnel cloud. I mean, it was scary and all that, but it was over an area of sugar beet fields and didn't seem to be a threat to anything. But it was awesome! It touched down and bounced up again and yo-yoed a while and finally just disappeared. One of the farmers in that area had a video camera and caught the whole thing on tape. He sent it in to the Weather Channel and they played it several times."

Palmer Knutson said, "When I was a kid they had that big tornado in Fargo. I think about thirteen people got killed. My dad was always curious about things like that and he would have gone there to look around the next day if my mother hadn't stopped him. When we finally did go to Fargo, it was a week later and you couldn't believe the damage. It was like some of those films of the German cities after World War II! I heard that forty miles to the east it actually rained furniture from Fargo."

And so it went, as story was piled upon story and the sky became very black.

Carla Sorgren held her husband's hand and noticed that Alan was becoming very nervous. She knew what he really wanted at this time, but hoped that she could keep him from making a solitary trip to his private stash. In truth, it was not the lack of a stimulant or even the storm that was making her husband nervous, it was something that he heard Kevin Charbonneau say. He had made the off hand comment that a tornado had once destroyed a meth lab in a trailer home in his county, and that the storm had actually done his office a favor. When he said so, he seemed to be looking directly at Alan. "Does he know?" Alan wondered. Then he looked at Harvey Green and saw him giving him a sly wink. *The bastard!* he thought. *He's telling everyone. One day I've got to take care of him once and for all.* He looked furtively at Carla. Had she seen the wink? He regretfully concluded that she had.

Harvey Green was boasting his county's disaster preparedness. *Big deal,* thought Ronnie Erstead. *A tornado might hit his county once every ten years and if it did, what did it matter if it blew down a few jack pines. He doesn't have to put up with floods, prairie fires, and half a dozen tornado watches every year. He's looking at me like he's saying, "You know, if I could administer that county, it would be in a lot better shape." And that sly look at Charbonneau seems to say, "You'll support me in this won't you?" And that young punk would be only too happy to.* He looked over to Denise and noted that she was probably thinking the same thing. Every time Green came up with yet another sappy story she seemed to sneer.

Green was boasting, "We got out to that storm scene within minutes of the tornado! If someone would have been injured, we could have taken care of him. Of course, I have a budget for just that kind of thing, and I make sure every nickel is accounted for."

Rather tartly, Ellie interjected, "Well, I'm sure you could have handled Hurricane Katrina better. But then, who couldn't?" Nobody seemed ready to pick up on this topic.

Brad Nichols, however, noticed that when Green was making his comment about accountability of funds, he was giving him what seemed to be a winking eye. Nichols thought, "He can't possibly know anything about my accounts, can he? Of course not! But as he thought this, Charbonneau added. "Yeah, I have heard stories about some sheriff's offices who use the disaster fund as their own little piggy bank. I mean, the money is supposed to be there, but if no disaster comes, I suppose there is a temptation to spend it somehow so that they can get an appropriation for the next year. How do you handle that, Brad? I mean, you haven't had anything like a disaster in your area for some time, have you?"

Nichols was obviously flustered. *What a weasel!* he thought. *But who cares what he thinks?* Then he noticed that Green was looking at him like a cat with a full bowl of cream. If anybody ever found out, his chances of leaving Hayes County would disappear.

Knutson was aware of the tension in the room. *Well, why wouldn't there be,* he thought to himself, *with a storm like that coming on. And yet, there's something more. As far as I know, nobody here has anything against me, but there is rancor in this room.*

At that moment, Charbonneau turned to Green and said, "Keeping track of funds and planning disaster assistance is one thing, but keeping track of prisoners in your jails can also be just murder, don't you think so, Harvey."

Knutson looked at Charbonneau just as the lightning flashed. Was that hatred? Or was he imagining things in the weird and artificial atmosphere? He rapidly looked at Green and thought he saw the same look in his eyes.

Meanwhile, Ellie did not seem to be paying too much attention to what she considered to be boring and fatuous communication. Nature was at its most cataclysmic state, and as she intently stared out at the low sky she shouted, "Look! Over there! It's a tornado!"

As she said this, the civil defense sirens began wailing. Still, no staff appeared to usher them to safer quarters, as every one of them, it seemed, was preoccupied in getting guests from the upper floors into the hotel lobby. The funnel cloud hung ominously at the end of the wall cloud, hesitated for about a minute, and then disappeared. Within minutes a gust of wind shook the hotel. Hailstones began to pummel the building while the ten lone occupants of the ballroom stepped back from the windows in case the hail would shatter the glass. For a few seconds, the electricity went out, but the room was almost constantly lit with dramatic lightning flashes that gave the impression of a massive strobe light. The rain came down with a sudden violence and lasted for about ten minutes. Then, quite unexpectedly, it stopped.

No one had spoken for several minutes and now the sheriff of Otter Tail County said, "Well, that was something, huh?"

To this profundity, no one dissented. Alan Sorgren, who seemed most anxious to get away, said, "I think I better go out and see if the hail did any damage to our car." Others mumbled that it was probably a good idea and began to file out of the room. At this point, the manager of banquet arrangements came into the room.

"Geez, are you still here? I thought we had everyone in one place for the tornado scare. Are you done in here?" He asked, looking suspiciously at the empty wine bottles on the table. "We've got to clean up."

Palmer noticed that no one had stepped forward to offer to pay for the wine. He decided he would mention it to Jason Two Bears. Or maybe not.

Back in their room, Palmer and Ellie went out on their balcony. Palmer put his arm around his wife as they watched a brilliant double rainbow form over Lake Bemidji. The scenery made Palmer think, as he always did, about his brother, Reverend Rolf Knutson, who consistently preached a yearly sermon on the story of Noah. It was pure poetry, and Palmer had listened to that sermon twenty times before he got around to asking his brother, "Do you really believe that there was a great flood and that Noah built a big ship to carry two of every kind of animal?" He was shocked when his brother said, "Well, of course not, but that does not detract from the glory of God's promise to man, does it? It just makes it a little easier for some people to understand."

Now, Palmer held his beloved wife in his arms. The storm was over, God was in his heaven, and all was right with the world.

In another part of the hotel, someone had just decided to commit murder.

Chapter Seven

P ALMER KNUTSON APPRECIATED A HOTEL that provided a coffee maker in the room. He always took advantage of it and was pleased to note the Radisson's choice of Starbuck's. Ellie, as usual, took longer to get ready in the morning, so Palmer took his coffee out to the balcony. The tasty brew served like a liquid defibrillator. In truth, it had not been an altogether restful night. He was awakened about two o'clock by the sound of sirens. His first thought was that the storm had returned, but as abruptly as the sirens had sounded, they became quiet again. He reasoned that it was a Bemidji police matter, and although his instinct was to get up and see what was happening, he decided that it wasn't his jurisdiction and that the local fuzz could handle it. It had taken him some time to get back to sleep. When he did sleep, he dreamed that he was in rural France. His plane had been shot down and the Nazis were searching for him. He had been wearing his uniform, but a laundry woman and an unguarded clothesline had provided him with a change in appearance. He was able to dodge the German patrols until he saw a man whom he thought must be a member of the *resistance*. "Are you American," the man asked. And Palmer had replied in impeccable French, *"Oui."*

As he gazed out on beautiful Lake Bemidji, he could not help but think that nothing could be further from the perils of World War II than Minnesota on a summer morning. The air seemed unbelievably fresh, as though the storm of the previous night had scoured the atmosphere of all impurities. He breathed deeply, noted with approval that someone was already out for an early sail on the lake, and sipped the delicious elixor of life. He was actually looking forward to the rest of the conference. This morning there would be a presentation by the Bureau of Criminal Apprehension concerning increased cooperation between the state and local levels of law enforcement. Then, following a nice coffee break, there would be the presentation by the local technicians from the BCA crime lab. Ever since that CBS series about *CSI*, the whole idea of forensic crime labs had been hot stuff. Palmer liked the show, although as a cop himself he was frequently dismayed by the preposterous elements of plot and procedure. Mostly, he liked the theme song, and he always sang along with Roger Daltry and the Who. Nevertheless, he mused, "It's becoming ridiculous. *Las Vegas*, then *CSI Miami*, then *CSI New York*. Can Minneapolis be far behind? Rochester? Moorhead? CSI Fergus Falls? He wondered what handsome Adonis would be chosen to play him.

The telephone rang, and since Ellie was still in the bathroom, he reluctantly went in to answer it himself. A pleasing idea occurred to him. Perhaps it was the media doing a story on last night's award. It was not.

"That you, Palmer? This is Jason Two Bears. I suppose you heard what happened last night. Do you think I should cancel the rest of the conference?"

Palmer was somewhat puzzled. "You mean because of the storm and people leaving early?"

"No, no, of course not. I mean the murder. My God, you mean you haven't heard?"

"I guess not. Who was murdered?"

"Oh, Gees. It was awful. I mean there's blood all over. The Bemidji police acted fast and got a perimeter around the scene, of course, but there's already been a steady stream of tourists. They come to see Paul Bunyan and instead they see a ring of cops and patrol cars. It's just gruesome."

"Jason! Who was murdered and why should it affect the conference?"

"Oh, sorry. Kevin Charbonneau was found with his throat cut and a carving knife sticking out of his belly. Did you know him?"

Palmer waited until the shock wore off before he said, "Kevin Charbonneau? Yah, I knew him, but not real well. In fact, we waited out the storm together last night. There were about ten of us sitting down in the ballroom watching the tornado. I was going to tell you about that, because . . ."

"Did he seem nervous? I mean, did he give any indication that his life may have been in danger?"

"Well, we all sort of felt that way at the time. We were watching a tornado, for heaven's sake! When and where did his happen?"

"The medical examiner determined, it happened around 1:30 a.m.. The reason he can be that exact is that when the body was discovered, it was still warm and the blood had not dried much. Four kids from Bemidji State University thought it would be a good idea to drink a six-pack while sitting under Babe the Blue Ox. Well, they're football players trying to make up some credits in summer school so they can play in the fall, what do you expect? Anyway, they were apparently feeling pretty good when they got to the statues, and were feeling real bad when they saw the body. One of 'em had a cell phone and called 911 at about 2:00 a.m."

"Two o'clock, huh? So that's what woke me up. There was a lot of noise from sirens."

"Yeah, I suppose. Look, I'm working with the Bemidji Police Department on this, so with your permission I'll tell them about how you rode out the storm with Charbonneau. You might have been one of the last people to see him alive. They might want to question you further about your impressions.

Meanwhile, what do you think we should do about the conference?"

Palmer noticed that Ellie had poked her head out from the bathroom and noticed the look of consternation on his face. Any call to the hotel room must surely be bad news about one of the kids! He managed to give a gentle downward wave of his hand to indicate that it was nothing for her to worry about. To Jason Two Bears he said, "Under the circumstances, I guess I'd say cancel it. I mean, if it were an ordinary murder it might not be necessary, but Kevin Charbonneau was one of us. Has anyone informed his wife? They haven't, or hadn't, I guess you'd say now, been married very long."

"I don't know. The Bemidji police said that they had no luck trying to reach his wife in their home, so they are conducting inquiries to see if anybody knows where she is. She was not staying with him at the conference, it seems. So, here's what I think I'll do. There's quite a group of people having breakfast or just hanging around the lobby. I'll just go down and pass the word around that the conference is cancelled so they can all go home."

With the wisdom of experience, Palmer urgently said, "No, Jason, don't tell them that. The police may want to talk to the conference participants."

"You're not thinking one of them had something to do with the murder?" Jason gasped.

"Probably not, although one can never assume anything. The most important thing, however, is that the Bemidji Police will be investigating this thing, and it'd look very bad if everyone lammed out of here, wouldn't it? It would seem on the face of it that the worst place to commit a murder would be in front of a hotel filled with sheriffs."

Knutson hung up the telephone and sat staring at the wall. Ellie, who had overheard the conversation, said, "Mur-

der? Here? And who is, or was, apparently, Kevin Charbonneau?"

Palmer stood shaking head and said, "He was that young
guy who sat around the table last night and made people feel
uncomfortable. I think he was the youngest sheriff in the
state. He was sheriff of Carson County."

Ellie said ruefully, "That handsome guy? What a shame!"

"You mean, if he had been a homely guy it would have
been all right?"

"Oh, Palmer, of course not! It just seems a shame that a
guy so young with so much life ahead of him, well, you
know. What are you going to do now?"

"Near as I can tell, there is nothing for me to do. Let's
go have breakfast."

Ellie straightened her skirt before the mirror and said,
"All right, but, Palmer? Can we go someplace other than the
hotel? All those colleagues of yours will be talking about the
murder. It's not a pleasant topic of conversation at breakfast."

"Yeah, sure. Where do you want to go?"

"Well," Ellie smiled, "there's always Paul's Pancake
House. You can have a real lumberjack breakfast. A stack
of flapjacks, sausage, butter, syrup—why, I can almost hear
your arteries moan in anticipation."

Smiling, Palmer lunged for the door. "Paul's pancakes it
is!"

As they passed through the lobby of the hotel, Palmer's
colleagues began to approach him, anticipating that he
would certainly have some news to share. Instead, however,
he held Ellie's arm as they stepped up the pace on their way
out. This was not the way Palmer had envisioned the morning. He felt somewhat cheated that the storm had cut short
the opportunity to bask in the glory of his award. He had
been looking forward to talking to old friends and accepting

their accolades. As a Norwegian-American, he could never have put himself forward to claim pats on the back, but if someone else did it, he could enjoy having his ego stroked as well as the next person. It was only a short walk to Paul's Pancake House, but by the time they got there, Palmer felt like he had left the problem behind.

* *

Rᴇᴛᴜʀɴɪɴɢ ᴛᴏ ᴛʜᴇ ʜᴏᴛᴇʟ, Palmer knew that he would pay for his excessive intake of calories and carbs. Fortunately, he had remembered to take along his antacid tablets. He slipped a couple of them in his mouth in the hopes that Ellie wouldn't see. It was a vain hope, and, predictably, she said, "It's been awhile since you had your last check-up isn't it, dear? You never used to be bothered by food like that."

"I didn't used to be this old, either," Palmer sourly replied.

Waiting for them by the Radisson's front entrance was Jason Two Bears. "Got a few minutes, Palmer?" He said.

"Yah, I suppose." He looked apologetically at Ellie and said, "Why don't you go on up to the room. I'll join you as soon as I know something."

Ellie smiled and said, "Sure, I'm used to being the wife of a sheriff." Privately, she was grateful that they had decided to have their night at Itasca before the conference and not afterward. Perhaps she couldn't console herself that they "would always have Paris," but "we'll always have Itasca" wasn't all that bad.

As soon as she was out of earshot, Knutson turned to Two Bears and said, "Yah, what's up?"

The sheriff of Beltrami County looked rather furtively at the others in the hotel lobby and said, "Come with me for a second. I want your opinion on something." Two Bears led him up the stairs to one of the rooms that would have been used for a conference presentation. As they pushed aside an overhead projector and sat down on a pair of stacking chairs in the corner of the room, Two Bears said, "The Bemidji Police think they have identified the murder weapon?"

Knutson leaned forward and said, "So soon? What is it?"

Again, Two Bears made a sly look at the door and said, "As I told you over the phone, they found the knife stuck in his stomach. Meaning there was never any doubt that it was at least one of the murder weapons. Whether the same knife was used to slit his throat as to stab him in the belly won't be known until later, but there is no reason to believe that it is not. The thing is, it is a rather specialized carving knife. No sooner had the word got around that someone had been murdered just across the street from the Radisson than the manager of the hotel saw the Bemidji cops in his restaurant and he asked to speak to Chief Mahony."

Palmer interrupted, "You're kidding. Mahony? Bemidji has an Irish chief of police? Mahony?"

"Two Bears scowled. "What's so funny about that?"

"Well, you know. The Irish cop. In everything from Dick Tracy to Batman they always have Irish cops. Next thing you're going to tell me is that they were all eating dough-nuts!"

"Well, as a matter of fact . . ."

"No!"

"Okay, they were muffins. But so what? The point is that the manager of the hotel tells Mahony that one of the knives from the carving set is missing. It is very sharp and it is very expensive. It is not something that someone would lose or mislay. The guy who was carving the prime rib for last night's banquet swears that the whole carving set remained in the banquet room during the storm last night and that when he went back later, apparently as soon as your group of storm watchers had left, the knife was not with the rest of the equipment. He said he noticed it right away because he always put the knife in a special slot at the side of his cutting board. At the time, he presumed some bus boy had taken it back to the kitchen and was, in fact, quite upset about it. When none of the bus boys would fess up to handling the knife, he was ticked off enough that he told the manager he should fire the lot of them until he could get someone he could trust. So this morning, when the manager hears about someone getting stabbed fifty yards from his hotel, he puts two and two together. He tells the chief and the chief calls up the meat carver, and they pick him up and take him to the police station. Sure enough, that guy identifies the knife. He says, 'It's a Wusthof. Just about the most expensive knife you can buy. I doubt if there's another one of these in all of Northern Minnesota.' Oh, and before you ask, there were no fingerprints. Whoever did this apparently came to the murder wearing rubber gloves."

Most pauses are not "pregnant." This one was. Finally, Two Bears said to Knutson, "You see what this means."

The flippancy with which Palmer greeted the news of the Irish chief of police was gone. He gave an odd little inward gasp and said, "You're not saying . . ."

"Yeah, I think I am. While it may not have been impossible for someone else to get in that room and pilfer that knife, the most likely time for it to have disappeared was when you were there. Tell me, did the lights ever go out?"

"Yah, for a short time."

"Were you distracted by the storm?"

"Are you kidding? We were watching a tornado funnel that could have touched down and wiped out the town. Of course we were distracted!"

"And do you think someone could have stolen the knife during that time?"

Palmer was aghast at the suggestion. "Hell, they could have stolen the whole damn carving cart!"

"But they did not. They stole a knife that could have been concealed in the inner pocket of a suit jacket or, perhaps, in some part of a dress."

"You're not suggesting that a woman . . ."

"As I recall, hearing about your murder cases in Fergus Falls . . ."

"Yah, you're right. Hooo boy! What are you going to do about it?"

Two Bears produced a somewhat humorless smile. "I'm not sure that I'm going to do anything about it. It's not my jurisdiction. This is a case for the Bemidji Police. I'm not sure that they want some Indian working on the case. I know of a couple of guys on that force, well, I guess they have retired now, but a couple of them would have regarded me as the most likely suspect. I mean, I was an Indian who was seen in the company of the victim. I think this has changed. No, in fairness, I know it has changed, but I've only had the job of "acting sheriff" for one week, so I'm not sure how big a part I'm going to have in all this. Of course, if I were offered the chance to be a part of the investigation, you know what I would be doing now, don't you?"

"What?"

"Interrogating you."

Palmer blinked. "Oh, yah, I suppose. Well then, perhaps it is a good thing that you will not be part of the investigation. Did you get any idea about when we will be allowed to go home?"

"Nope, but I'll keep in touch."

* *

Palmer returned to his room to find Ellie watching politics on MSNBC. "I love Ed Schutz," she said as Palmer entered the room, "I had to miss him last night. Apparently he was attacking Rush Limbaugh, whom he calls 'the Drugster.'" I sometimes wonder if any of those guys on Fox ever really care what they say, or whether they are just after ratings. The more outrageous things they say, the more attention they get. By the way, do you think we can go home soon?"

"I don't know," Palmer wheezed, as he sat beside her on the bed. "Jason didn't seem to know anything about that. But guess what? Apparently, the murder weapon was the carving knife that guy was using on the prime rib last night. The Bemidji cops seem to think one of the ten people who were in that room during the storm took it. How's that for a thought. 'One of us is the murderer.' I can just see Inspector Clouseau delivering that line!"

"Well, if it is any comfort to you, I didn't take it."

"Hmmmm, there goes my prime suspect. So, since I know I didn't take it, and you claim, although you offer no proof, that you didn't take it, that would seem to narrow the list of suspects to eight, no wait, seven, since it is apparent that Charbonneau did not commit suicide. But suppose . . ."

At that moment, the telephone rang. Palmer looked at Ellie and when she made no move to answer it, he picked up the receiver and uttered a curt "yah?"

"Palmer, Jason here. It turns out I'm calling you sooner than I expected. I Just met with Chief Mahony. He said that since the whole conference was my show, he wants me to be part of the investigation. 'White of him,' as I've actually heard people say. Really, though, I'm rather honored that he has done so. He sent Lieutenant Jack Hanson over here and he and I are going to take charge of the interviewing. We decided that we should just make sure we have the name and address of everyone here at the hotel and with a few obvious exceptions, let 'em all go home. To be sure there's still the possibility that someone from outside the hotel is the killer, but the nature of the murder weapon does seem to point to a connection with someone at the hotel. Nevertheless, it seems that it would be a professional courtesy not to keep fellow law enforcement personnel here longer than necessary. We are, however, going to spend part of today interviewing all of you who spent the final hours of Charbonneau's life in his company. Bottom line, I really do want to interview you and your wife. Of course, since you are the senior sheriff, we'd like to talk to you first. Not only because you are the oldest, of course, but also because you are more experienced and, let's face it, I value your opinion more than the rest of them put together. So, when can we start?"

Palmer listened intently to all of this and with a glance over at Ellie, said, "As far as I'm concerned, the sooner the better. Who do you want to talk to first, me or Ellie?"

At the mention of her name, Ellie's eyes widened. She mouthed a questioning "Me?"

Two Bears said, "I think we should talk to you first. It might make grilling Ellie easier."

Palmer thought, *There was humor in that statement, wasn't there?* Aloud he said, "Okay, where should I go?"

"Since the conference booked that room we were just in, we've decided that it can be used as an incident room. We'll be talking to everyone there. So, in about ten minutes?"

"All right, I'll be there," said Palmer, scowling as he hung up the phone.

Chapter Eight

P
ALMER KNUTSON HAD NEVER BEEN on the other side of an
interrogation before, and even though he knew he had
nothing to fear, he found himself becoming nervous. As
he walked into the room he noticed Jason Two Bears looking somewhat stern. He hoped it was just a case of putting
on a face for the Bemidji police officer. As the officer, dressed
in plain clothes, stood, Two Bears said, "Um, Palmer, this is
Lieutenant Jack Hanson, of the Bemidji Police Department.
Jack, Palmer Knutson, sheriff of Otter Tail County."

As Hanson shook Palmer's hand he said, "Yeah, Palmer
Knutson, I've heard a lot about you."

Palmer, trying to keep things light, said, "All good, I hope."

"Absolutely. Jason here says you might be able to tell us
something about the last few hours in the life of Kevin Charbonneau. Have a seat. Need some coffee?"

Palmer sat heavily and said, "No thank you. My tonsils
are already singing 'Anchors Aweigh!' I guess I'd like to get
this over with. Jason said you would also like to interview
my wife, and then I suppose we would like to put an egg in
our shoe and beat it."

Hanson sat down and nodded to Two Bears. "Right. We
are going to tape this, just to keep a record of our investigation. I presume you don't mind?"

This was another new experience for Palmer. He would
not be on the questioning end of a taped interview. "Nope.
Go ahead," he tersely replied.

"Now, Jason has told you about the significance of the
time that the ten of you spent in the banquet room last night.

That is, it seems that the murder weapon was there at the time that everyone else cleared out and was gone after your group left. We would like to know everything that you can remember about that period. I presume you did not see anyone take the knife, or you would have told us. I am also reasonably sure that you did not take the knife yourself. I hesitate to call any of you suspects, but at this stage of the investigation we just need to gather whatever information we can and see if we can establish or rule out motives, means, and opportunities. Well, you know the drill. Start at the beginning and tell us whatever you can about that period."

"So you really think it is possible that one of us in that room, including six county sheriffs, or five, since one is now a corpse, is a murderer? If that's the case, you should probably be treating that ballroom as a crime scene."

Two Bears gave a slight grimace and Palmer noticed a strained expression on the face of the policeman. Hanson said, "Look, Knutson, try not to tell us how to do the job, huh? Just answer the questions. As it happens, the ballroom has been sealed and we are treating it as a part of our investigations."

Palmer's face took on the aspect of one who had just eaten the last cookie. "Yah, um, sorry. I didn't mean to, you know, um. All right, start the tape and I'll tell you what I can remember about last night." Palmer paused and heard the familiar click of a tape recorder. "We were all at the banquet and then we get word that we're under a tornado warning. Ellie and I were at the head table and people kept coming up and shaking my hand and so we got sort of a late start in getting out of there. Before we knew it—I mean the place was emptied out in five minutes, I'm sure—we were alone with eight other people. There was Harvey Green, sheriff of Green County, Alan Sorgren, sheriff of Monroe County and his wife, um, um, Carla, I think her name is, Ronnie and Denise Erstead, he's sheriff of Harrison County, Brad Nichols, who's sheriff of Hayes County, and his wife, Karen, and, of course, Kevin Charbonneau."

"Do you know why these individuals chose to stay in the ballroom instead of leaving like everyone else?"

Palmer thought and after a short hesitation said, "I can only speak for myself and Ellie, of course, but we stayed just to watch the storm come in. I've always been fascinated by things like that, and our hotel room faced the other way. I figured that if a tornado did hit the hotel, we could spot it in plenty of time to take shelter. And we did see it, as it turned out, even if it never touched down. I think that was the main reason why the others stayed, too, although perhaps Green and Charbonneau, who did not have their wives along, were just looking for some company. In any event, we just sat there watching the storm and talking sheriff stuff.

"Sheriff stuff?"

"Yah. You know, common problems, emergency preparedness, stuff like that. We also talked about other tornados that we had seen. It all seems pretty mundane as I look back on it."

"Now think back, if you can," Hanson said, in a manner that Knutson considered to be a patronizing recognition of his advanced age, "can you remember any conversations that would have seemed to be threatening or comments that were made that could have upset anyone? We're just trying to get the dynamics of that night."

Palmer scratched his belly and then his head. "Well, I remember that Harvey Green was making some exaggerated comments on the effects of tornados. But that's Harvey, you know. He's always full of . . . Oh, I forgot, this is on tape. Anyhow, just about everyone, including myself, put in their two cents worth of tornado stories."

Hanson leaned in and said, "Did any member of that gathering seem especially nervous?"

Palmer said, "Jason asked that earlier. I'll say again that I just assumed that we were all a little jumpy as we watched those clouds. As I recall, the conversation seemed to drift from storm stories to how the various departments were prepared to handle disasters. I remember someone talking about the response to Hurricane Katrina, I'm not sure who that was, and then people talked about county budgets for preparedness. I seem to remember Green bragging about his readiness and kind of hinting that maybe Brad Nichols wasn't. But I didn't get the feeling of any deep animosity or anything like that. I don't know, we just talked about things, then Ellie spotted the tornado, then everyone shut up for a while. Pretty soon it was all over and then we all left the room."

"Can you remember where people were standing during this time?" Hanson asked. "I mean, you know, did you happen to notice, for instance, if anyone was near the carving cart?"

"Yah, I've been thinking about that ever since Jason told me where the knife came from. I just remember we were all sitting around this big table, drinking wine and talking, and then at some point we all got up and stood next to the window. Now that I think of it, Ellie must have left the table a little earlier, because she was the one that spotted the funnel cloud. Maybe she was standing there with another woman. Maybe Karen Nichols, but I can't be sure. Anyway, as I recall, once she yelled that she saw the tornado, we all got up and crowded around. There we were, looking out the window and all in a line, which means that someone must have been on the end near the carvery. But, I mean, you're looking out at a funnel cloud that may just touch down where you are standing and you don't take roll as to where people are. So, not long after that the big wind hits the hotel and then the rain comes down in sheets and hail starts bouncing off the windows and we all took a step back. It was at this time that the lights went out for a short time, and I far as I can remember, we all pretty much stood still until they came back on. I'm not sure if anyone ever sat down again. The whole storm ended kind of abruptly and the next thing you knew we were out of there. I'm afraid that's all I can tell you."

Hanson sighed and after a bit reached over and turned off the recorder. "Okay, but keep thinking about it. Maybe something will come back to you later, something that didn't seem significant at the time but that now, in light of what happened, may mean something." Palmer nodded, thinking about all the times he had told a potential witness exactly the same thing. "Here, here's my card. Call me, or Jason, of course, if you think of anything else. As far as I'm concerned, after we have talked to your wife, you can go home. We know where we can get a hold of you if we need to."

Palmer stood and said, "Sure thing. Thanks. Um, before Ellie comes in, I'd like a short word with Jason."

Jason led Palmer out of the room and to the edge of the hotel lobby. "Got something else to tell me that you didn't want on tape?" Jason asked.

Knutson looked embarrassed. "Yah, do you think, I mean, if you edit that tape, that you could take out that reference to drinking wine?"

Two Bears looked surprised. "Why? Don't you want the good citizens of Otter Tail County to believe that their sheriff actually has a little wine now and then?"

"No, of course not. It's just that, well, I found those four opened bottles of wine on the bar and no one was around and I, well, I just I swiped them. Now of course I want to pay for them, so if you can just ask the hotel to send me the bill."

Two Bears smiled. "Palmer, you are too honest for your own good. Since the bottles were already opened, I have a feeling that the hotel would find a way to charge the conference for them anyway. And if they do? So what! We'll take care of it."

Knutson looked relieved. "Okay. Thanks. I'll send Ellie in, if you are ready for her."

Two Bears smiled, "You do that, Palmer, and have a good trip home."

* *

PALMER TOOK THE ELEVATOR TO HIS ROOM, noting, with annoyance, "The Girl From Ipanema" playing on the speaker. He entered the room and said to Ellie, "They told me to tell you that they are ready to talk to you. It won't take long at all, since I already told them everything. While you're gone, I'll take the luggage down to the car and check out. I'll be back here watching CNN if you are still talking to those guys when I'm done."

Ellie said, nervously, "Well, is it, um, scary to be interrogated?"

"Interrogated? Nah! They just ask you what you saw last night. Don't worry about it. You can even have a cup of coffee if you'd like."

When Ellie left, Palmer took one final look around the room and lugged the bags down to the car, smugly opening the trunk lid with his remote control. Although it was no longer an uncommon luxury, it never ceased to amaze him. He shuffled back to the hotel lobby, stopping to glance across the road to where the Bemidji police had set up a perimeter with yellow tape. Palmer assumed that they would do everything in their power to speed up that procedure. People didn't want to have their picture taken with a blue ox if the blue ox was surrounded by scene-of-the-crime tape. On the other hand, he reflected, they probably did.

Ellie was not waiting for him in the lobby, so he went back to the room and turned on the television. "Whoops," Britney Spears seemed to have "done it again." He turned the channel to get a repeat of the *Colbert Report*, since he had missed it the night before. He appreciated being part of the "Colbert Nation," and the time passed pleasantly. When it ended, Ellie had still not returned. The "Repore" was followed by *South Park*, but since that was too much for Palmer, he went back to CNN, all the while getting more eager to leave. Finally, almost an hour after she had gone, Ellie softly knocked on the door and said, "Palmer? Are you still here?"

Palmer opened the door and said, "I'm sorry, sweetheart, I don't need maid service, but if you see my wife, can you tell her I'm still waiting? Are you ready to go now? What took you so long?"

Ellie walked with Palmer down to the elevator and told him "I just answered their questions. They were quite nice about the whole thing. You didn't tell me that they would record everything I said. That was kind of off-putting. But I got used to it, I suppose. I guess it did take longer than I thought it would, but they were very thorough, I thought."

Privately, Palmer thought to himself *Yah, I bet. I suppose they just asked a simple question and, like a woman, you went on and on. We men are so superior when it comes to just giving the information necessary and then shutting up!* Out loud, he said, "I'm sure you did just fine."

When they were leaving the parking lot, Ellie asked, "Can we go home by way of Leech Lake and Walker? That's such a pretty drive. Is it too much longer?"

Palmer considered this for a moment and said, "No, it's not too much longer, and we don't have any reason to hurry to get back to Fergus Falls, do we? I can just stay on Highway 2 until we get to Cass Lake and then take 371 South. Good idea."

Palmer reached toward the radio and Ellie thought, *Oh, no. He's going to turn on that dreadful "oldies" station again.*

Instead, Palmer pressed the button for CDs and pressed selection six. As he looked over to Ellie, he noted her questioning look. *Ah,* he thought, *I'll bet she thinks I'm going to play Jethro Tull music.* Aloud, he said, "I bought a new CD that I've been saving for a nice drive through the lake country. To tell you the truth, I was going to play it in Itasca Park, but it was so nice and quiet there I, well, I guess I sort of forgot about it."

Ellie braced herself and asked, "What is it?"

"It's a new recording by the London Symphony of Camille Saint-Saens 'Carnival of the Animals.'"

"Oh, Palmer. I love that."

"Yes, I know you do. And that's one of the reasons I bought it. But I like it too, you know. In fact, I was doing a little research on Saint-Saens before I bought it. I learned that he was just about as much as a child prodigy as Mozart. No joke, he started playing the piano when he was two years old, and when he was three and a half he produced his first piano composition. Amazing guy, apparently. I mean, Mozart was sort of an 'idiot savant,' that is, although he was smart enough, he was a genius only in music. Saint-Saens, on the other hand, was really exceptional in all areas. He learned Latin by age seven, studied geology and archeology, was an advanced mathematician, wrote a book on his own view of philosophy which was sort of existential, and he was also a playwright. Oh, yah, he also had his own telescope made to order so he could better study astronomy!"

"Wow!" Ellie said, "He might have been smart enough to be a county sheriff."

"Well, probably not that smart! For instance, he really didn't appreciate his own work. After 'Carnival of the Animals' was introduced in 1886, or some time around there, he never even published the thing. In fact, the whole composition wasn't published until after he died, some thirty-five years later."

"He lived about the same time as Ravel, didn't he?"

"Yep, but apparently they didn't like each other. I suppose Saint-Saens thought Ravel's music to be too exciting. You gotta admit, this is pretty mellow stuff. Here, listen to this. This is 'The Swan.' Listen to that cello! Now that's sweet!"

With this "mellow cello" filling the interior of the Acura, they made their way pleasantly back to Fergus Falls.

Chapter Nine

I T WAS SUNDAY MORNING, AND PALMER AND ELLIE sat in an inconspicuous pew in the middle of the First Norwegian Lutheran Church for the eleven o'clock service. There was no need to go earlier, as it was not football season, with its looming noon kickoff for the Vikings. Earlier that morning. Palmer experienced one of the joys of his life, which was sitting on his deck with a cup of coffee and completing the *New York Times* crossword puzzle, faithfully presented by the *Minneapolis Star Tribune*. It was time to do penance for luxury.

The First Norwegian Lutheran Church was a massive brown brick building, with a square tower crowned by the tallest steeple in Fergus Falls. The interior was tastefully but modestly covered by oak paneling and featured a simple but elegant altar, behind which stood an old painting of a rising Christ. Perhaps even more elegant and impressive was the carved pulpit, now dominated by the Reverent Rolf Knutson. Pastor Knutson had been called the Western Minnesota Lutheran pope, not because of any high church sympathies, but because of the manner in which he dominated the affairs of his synod. He was a magnificent figure of a man, with a flowing mane of white hair that gave him a demeanor that could only be described as leonine. His magnificent voice, powerful and yet comforting, could reach the farthest corner of an auditorium. It was a voice that Palmer once said, "carried like a pigeon," a simile which Rolf did not find amusing. In the pulpit he seemed to be seven feet tall, and Palmer was always surprised that when he stood next to his older brother, he was actually about an inch taller.

The text for the day was Mathew 5:16. "Let your light so shine before men, that they may see your good works and give glory to your Father who is in heaven." It was a text he preached upon at least once a year, and although familiar, Reverend Knutson always found some new meaning to make it current. Palmer reflected on one of the few times he had discussed theology with his brother. "It's a good text," Rolf had told him, because it speaks to us about our every-day life. Of course, it is also a very conservative text."

"How so?" Palmer asked.

"Well, think about it. It was one of Luther's favorite top-ics—the dignity of the Christian man, the freedom of the Christian man. Luther preached that whatever one's station in life, we must glorify God."

"All right," Palmer said, "but why is that so conserva-tive?"

"Keep in mind that Luther never left the church," Rolf continued. "He was kicked out of it. He never considered himself to be a revolutionary. Of course, in retrospect, we can see the Reformation as one of the most radical and rev-olutionary acts for a thousand years. But Luther never sought a massive social reform. In fact, when the peasant's revolt broke out in the 1520s, Luther wrote a tract entitled 'Against the Murdering and Thieving Hordes of Peasants!' Basically Luther was saying that whatever one's vocation, he should be satisfied with it and be able to live that vocation in the service of God."

"Again, why is that so conservative?" Palmer asked.

"Don't you see? He's telling everyone to know his place in the world. Don't rise above your station. Be content with your lot in life. Now, that might have played well to the con-gregations of sixteenth-century Germany, but how do you think it would go over in modern America? Perhaps I should stand up in the pulpit and tell all the farm kids that they shouldn't go to college but merely be content with the plow for the rest of their lives. Furthermore, Luther solidly backed the powers that be. What do you think the reaction would be if I told everybody they should shut up and do what the president told them to do? I'd be offending either Democrats or Republicans, depending on what the president was. So I've adapted that text, and I do so every year. Now you, Palmer, are a fine sheriff. In that capacity, let your light shine."

Well, it was a sort of humbling thing to hear, and Palmer had nodded and mumbled that he would try to do his best.

Rolf would have none of it. "I'm not preaching to you, Palmer. I'm not doing the 'brother's keeper' thing. I'm just explaining why I do it. For what it's worth, I think you let your light shine every day."

Reflecting on that discussion now, Palmer remembered that it had made him feel pretty good. *What is it about the tyranny of family,* he thought, *that can make an older brother seem like someone that one had to please? Whatever!* He realized that he had tuned out to what Rolf was saying, but instead of getting back to listening to the sermon, he found himself thinking about the "calling" to be a county sheriff. And that made him think about the events of the weekend. To be sure, he had never killed anyone, but if indications were true, one of the five currently breathing sheriffs were in that room at the Radisson Hotel, or one of their spouses, had killed a man. He knew he hadn't done it, and he knew Ellie hadn't done it, so that left seven other people. What could be farther from "letting your light shine" as a county sheriff than viciously murdering someone?

"Could it be Allan or Carla Sorgren?" He thought. *"If so, why?"* Both of them looked a little antsy, in retrospect, but then, he reflected, he didn't really know them that well. The same with Ronnie and Denise Erstead. Sure, one might say

that he was stuck in a dead-end job on the prairie, but why would they want to off Charbonneau. Clearly there was more here than met the eye. Or Brad or Karen Nichols. He knew them fairly well, and a more mild couple he could hardly imagine. That left Harvey Green. *"Now there's a possibility,"* he thought. On the other hand, was that just a case of thinking that because he really didn't like the man and he would prefer to see him be the murderer? He reflected back to some of his other cases, and remembered that many times the most unlikely suspect had been the perpetrator. *Nevertheless*, he silently reminded himself, *It's not my case. I'm sure Jason Two Bears and Lieutenant Hanson can handle it just fine.*

He was suddenly jabbed in the ribs by Ellie, who was trying to pass him the collection plate. Palmer blinked in bewilderment, then automatically reached in his pocket for his envelope.

* *

THE NEXT MORNING AS HE ENTERED his office, he noticed that Orly Peterson was already busy with the county's business. He stopped at the coffee machine, filled his Minnesota Twins mug, and walked into Orly's office without knocking—a practice he had learned from Orly—and sat down. Orly looked, as usual, as though he had just returned from modeling uniforms for an article in *Gentleman's Quarterly*.

"So, did you make it back to your lake house all right on Friday night?"

"Yeah, but I'm glad we left when we did. We barely got in the cabin when the storm hit. Allysha's mother was kind of shook up. That's about as black as I've ever seen the clouds, lightning all over, hail, and a wind that almost blew the boat off the rack. I heard there was a funnel cloud near Bemidji. Did you see it?"

"Yup. Sure did. It looked like it was going to come down and hit the town, but it just went back up in the clouds and fizzled out."

"You sound like you're disappointed."

"No, of course not, but you know, those things really are something."

Peterson agreed that they were, then said, "So, are you going to be doing anything with that investigation into the murder?"

"Nah," Palmer said. "They can handle it. Besides, I'm sort of a suspect, you know, since I was one of the last people to see Charbonneau alive. Did you ever meet him?"

Orly thought for a moment and said, "No, I don't think I ever did. In fact, I don't think I've ever been in Carson County. How about you?"

Palmer nodded, "Yah, I guess I met him a couple of times. But he was many years younger, you know, so I didn't really know him very well. I did know his father, though, because he ran a little fishing resort up on Lake Grundorf, sort of the competition to the Grundorf Pines Resort. One year, about twenty years ago now, my brother thought he needed a fishing vacation and rented a cabin from him. I went up there and visited him not long before it closed.

"You might have heard about why it closed—nasty situation! Louis Charbonneau was murdered and they never did find out who had done it. Kevin Charbonneau was just a kid at the time and I always got the impression that he went into criminal justice as a kind of, oh, I don't know, a crusade to catch criminals like the ones who killed his dad. Like Bruce Wayne did, you know. Charbonneau—the younger one who got himself murdered this weekend, that is—was kind of a humorless sort, I always felt. Still, not to speak ill of the dead, eh?"

Orly furled his brow and squinted. "Bruce Wayne?"

Palmer grinned triumphantly, "Batman, of course."

"Oh, right. So when is the funeral?"

"I don't know. I suppose they'll let us know."

"Are you going to go?" Orly asked.

"I don't know. I suppose I'll have to. I'm not big on funerals, but he was a fellow sheriff and we did spend part of his last night together. I suspect that all the other county sheriffs will be there and it'll reflect rather poorly on our department if I don't go. Somebody always finds a way to make a big deal out of things like this. I mean, I wouldn't be surprised if our smarmy governor wasn't there, ready to turn tragedy into an opportunity to do politicking. At least, that's what Ellie says, although I suspect that, if he were not a Republican, she'd see his presence as heroic. Wanna come along?"

Orly smiled complacently and shook his head. "Of course, I'd consider it an honor and duty to attend, but if you go, well, somebody should be here in charge of the office. I'm willing to let you represent the department."

"That's magnanimous of you," Palmer said sarcastically. "Remind me to write that up in your year-end review. What's on for this week? Anything pressing?"

Orly made a pretense of shuffling some papers and then looked up and said, "Nah, we have some papers to serve, a farm eviction—those are never pleasant. There's a summer festival in Perham, with a parade on Saturday, so I suppose we'll have to show the flag there a bit. Someone broke into some cabins on Otter Tail Lake, and I've sent Chuck Schulz to look into it . . ."

"Chuck Schultz? That's a case that won't get solved."

"I know, but I figured it was something that he couldn't botch up too badly and we've got to give him something to do. In any event, it's always fun to read his reports. He puts so much into them, and they're just a hoot."

As he left Orly and walked into his own office, Palmer chuckled. As he sat down and tried to think of something useful to do, he began to consider, "Should I wear a suit or my uniform to that funeral. I wonder what the other sheriffs will wear?"

Chapter Ten

O N Sunday morning, Acting Sheriff Two Bears drove along the western shore of Lake Bemidji. Jack Hanson put in motion the investigative routine of the Bemidji Police Department and there seemed to be little he could do to add to their effort. In a high profile case such as this, the attention of the whole state was on them. The *Minneapolis Star Tribune* trumpeted "Sheriff Murdered at Sheriffs' Convention" and he had been obliged to set up a press conference to answer several questions that dripped with sensational undertones. The case made CNN, MSNBC, and Fox News, with coverage that was lurid and sensational. He was almost expecting to be featured in "News of the Weird."

Jason had told his wife, Lin, to ignore the land line and answer only the cell phone. If, by chance, any reporter happened to get that number, Jason told her to simply say that she had no comment. He hated to have her face that kind of pressure only a week after he had been on the job. And the job now seemed more difficult than ever. He still drove his eleven-year-old Toyota Corolla, but he wondered if it might be time for a change. *This thing still runs like a top,* he said to himself, *but how much longer? When they made me acting sheriff, nobody ever got around to mentioning money. But I should get a raise, shouldn't I. To be sure, nobody had the authority to mention it at the time, but the County Commission is supposed to meet in a couple of weeks, and maybe I should see if they have even thought about it. Besides, I should be driving the Beltrami County Sheriff's car, if we could only find out where Neil put the keys. I suppose if I drove that all the time, we could just keep this little Corolla, trusty as it is. That way, Lin could drive to her school and wouldn't have to walk all the time.* Jason smiled as he thought of giving Lin a ride to Hubert Humphrey Elementary School every morning and her insistence on walking the two miles home every afternoon. He smiled broader as he thought of just how good a shape it kept her in and began to wonder if giving her the Corolla was such a good idea after all.

Soon, however, he was concentrating on the problem at hand. The interviews with the "suspects," the county sheriffs and their wives, had raised more questions than they had answered. All mentioned snippets of conflict and one of the interview subjects had been amazingly concise and observant. He decided he needed help and he had determined that the only one to give him that help was a thousand miles away in Saskatchewan.

As he entered the Beltrami County Law Enforcement Center, he was delighted to see Deputy Milt Johnson already hard at work. "Hey, Milt, what's up?" he asked.

Johnson replied, "Am I glad to see you! The phone has been ringing ever since I got here. I presume you have a huge number of callers on your voice mail, and I just got off the phone with somebody from the B.B.C. The B.B.C., for God's sake!"

"Does that mean that you are going to be on the radio in England?"

Johnson smiled ruefully and said, "To tell you the truth, I was kind of hoping that would be it. Basically, they just wanted to talk to you. They are all exited about the Native American Sheriff investigating. We always seem to fascinate them. Oh, and do you know when the funeral will be? Everybody wants to know."

"No, but that's what I want to find out as soon as possible. I'm sure that many of the callers I've had are asking that question. I'd like to know where things stand before I get around to returning all those calls. But first, I want to see if I can contact Neil."

Two Bears went directly to his office and switched on his computer. He "googled" "Aurora Borealis Fishing Camp" and found a number. He tried to calculate what would be the best time to catch his erstwhile boss. It was now nine o'clock—eight o'clock in Saskatchewan. Neil Meyer had never struck him as a "morning person," and it might still be cold on the lake at that time of the morning. Neil, as he recalled, never liked the cold. Therefore, it would be more like Neil to be having breakfast, the only really good time to catch him. Jason consulted his notes, hoped for the best, and dialed the number.

"Good Morning, Aurora Borealis Fishing Camp," replied a chirpy voice.

Jason cleared his throat and said, "Yes, I wonder if you have a guest registered there by the name of Neil Meyer?"

"Neil? Oh, boy do we ever. Wanna talk to him?"

"Er, yes, that's why I called."

"Hang on! I'll see if he's conscious."

After a long wait, accompanied by unidentified noises on the other end, Jason heard a somewhat frightened, "Hello?"

Jason responded with a cheery, "Hi, Neil, this is Jason." The tradition of generations does not disappear rapidly. Jason could no more have jumped immediately to the point of his telephone call than he could have attended a John Wayne film festival. It was, to his sensitivities, rude. He began, therefore, with a polite inquiry. How's the fishing up there?"

"Huh? Oh, it's great. Been out every day since we got here. This is some lake! It's huge! You should see the waves. And cold? You gotta get all bundled up before you get out there. Luckily, I always have something along to warm me up internally, if you know what I mean. We get on this big boat, they provide the bait, and we can hardly put a line in the water before we get a fish. I mean, we're talking lunkers! The water is so damn cold that you certainly don't want to go in after them. Uffda! But, hey, I'm sure you didn't just call me just to talk fishing. Is there anything the matter with my family?"

Jason hurried to inform him that there was not, but thought that he had better come to the point. "I don't suppose you have heard the news from Bemidji?"

Meyer exploded impatiently, "I haven't heard the news from any place. Hell, we could be in the middle of a nuclear attack and I wouldn't know it. That's one of the reasons I wanted to come up here. Why, what's happened?"

Jason calmly explained, "There's been a murder. It's gotten a lot of publicity because it happened at the sheriff's conference. The press is playing up the irony angle and it has been all over the national news."

"Oh, my gosh! Who got killed?"

Jason described the events of the last two days in an orderly and logical fashion. There is always a relationship to one's former boss. If one likes him, one tries to live up to his expectations, if one despises him, one tries to show him up. For Jason, it was the former. It was not really a case of seeking Meyer's approval, he thought, but then reflected that perhaps that was somewhat the situation. In any event, as he concisely summed up the case, Meyer could not help but feel a sense of pride in his successor.

When Two Bears was finished, Meyer said, "Boy, you sure got your hands full on the first week on the job, but I'm sure you can handle it. If there's anything I can do, don't hesitate to ask."

This was, after all, why Jason had called. He said, "As a matter of fact, there is something you can do. First, can you tell me where you put the keys to the car?"

Meyer said, "Yah, sure. But I didn't mean to take 'em. I drove my own car up to Hector Airport in Fargo and left it in the long-term lot. I totally forgot I had the keys to the sher-iffmobile on the same key ring. Can you get along without them until I get back?"

The habitual amiability was reflected in Jason's voice as he said, "Sure. No problem. But that's not what I had in mind. You see, we're getting a lot of help on this case. In fact, the sheriff's office and the Bemidji police are doing a joint investigation—"

"Who you working with?" Meyer interrupted.

"Jack Hanson. You know him?"

"Yeah, known him since we called him Jackie Hanson. He's a good man. Anybody else?"

"Well, this is where it could get sticky. Because it is high profile, the F.B.I. thinks they should have a piece of the ac-tion, and since a law enforcement official was murdered, the Minnesota Office of the Department of Homeland Security is looking into it just in case it involves a secret army of ter-rorists making their first strike in Bemidji, Minnesota."

Again Meyer interrupted. "Do you know the guy who's head of that? He's some crony of the governor. If he hands you what he says is Shinola, well, don't put it on your shoes, if you know what I mean."

Jason chuckled and said, "Point taken and thanks for the warning. But I've been following a line of investigation that the others seem to be ignoring. Let me tell you about my "prime suspects."

Two Bears described the conditions in the Radisson ball-room on the night of the storm and the disappearance of what would prove to be the murder weapon. One by one he summarized the interviews of those "prime suspects" and his intuitive feelings that multiple motives certainly did exist. When he had finished the summary, he said, "So you see, what I need to do is investigate my colleagues. This is clearly skating on thin ice, especially since only one is guilty, while each one had the means and the opportunity. I'll have to live with and cooperate with whoever is not associated with the murder. Basically, it is a case of investigating them without their knowing that they're being investigated. Therefore, I need contacts. People I can call and ask in confidential circumstances about the other sheriffs, and their wives, and not have it get back to them. I figured that you were in office a long time and you could give me a few names. If you want me to, I can keep your name out of it."

There was a long silence on the other end of the line until Meyer finally said, "Yeah, I see what you mean, and I've been thinking about a few names as you were speaking. I can see where you would want to keep my name out of it, but in fact, it might be helpful in many of the cases if you used my name. They might not know you, but they know me, and they might be more willing to tell you what you need to know. Got a pencil ready?"

＊＊＊＊＊＊＊＊＊＊＊＊＊＊＊＊＊＊＊＊＊＊＊＊＊＊＊＊＊＊＊＊＊

Twenty minutes later, Sheriff Two Bears had a list and a direction. None of it might be of any use. In fact, he might be following a blind trail and look incompetent while the F.B.I. or the Bemidji Police Department solved the case. He made a lot of calls that Sunday, and spent a lot of time on the Internet, using the magic of search engines. On Monday, he made more calls, all the while discovering things that, in retrospect, he would rather not have known. He had amassed an ocean of information, much of it sensitive, much of it speculative, and some of it, perhaps, wrong and even slanderous. This was the kind of information that he did not want to hand off to other investigators, but he sure needed to talk to somebody. The sheriff of Otter Tail County had asked to be informed as to the date and time of the funeral. He took a deep breath and called Palmer Knutson.

* *

PALMER KNUTSON JUST DECIDED to wear a suit to the funeral when the telephone rang. He heard a voice filled with a bit of trepidation that said, "Er, Sheriff Knutson? This is Jason Two Bears."

Knutson said, "Jason. Good to hear from you. How ya doing? Have they set the date for the funeral yet?"

"Well, that's one of the reasons why I called. First of all, the funeral for Kevin Charbonneau will be held in his hometown of Durham on Wednesday morning. It will be at Saint Joseph's Catholic Church at 11:00 a.m. It looks like it's gonna be a big deal. Jack Hanson told me this morning that the governor is planning to attend." *No surprise there,* thought Knutson. "But secondly, I was wondering, um, you know, since you might be passing through Bemidji on the way to Durham anyway, you know, if, uh, you could spend a little time with me. I've got this little house on Lake Bemidji, used to belong to my wife's family, and there's room for you, and your wife if she'd like to come along, and we can go boating. Do you like to water ski? Or maybe go out and drown some worms and have a beer or two or three. It's just that, well, the Bemidji police don't seem to be getting very far, and I've come up with some leads that I'm not yet ready to share with them, and you have had more experience than I have. Some of the information I've gathered is really quite sensitive, and I'd just like to pick your brain about what to do with it and what it could mean. Furthermore, I've got a lead on something about Charbonneau, but it's from a source who insists on speaking only with you.

"Really," Palmer scowled, "who could that be?"

"Well, I'd rather not discuss this on the phone. But I'd like your input about what, if anything, I should do with this information. What do you think?

"I was just talking about the funeral with my deputy, and yah, I guess I'd better put in an appearance. And yah, I suppose I would be going through Bemidji anyway. I think I might be in a parade in Perham on Saturday—as you may discover, it is good politics never to miss a local festival—but I presume whatever we need to do can be wrapped up by then. I doubt if I would be up for skiing, though. It's been a long time since I've been on water skis, I'm not even sure a pair of water skis could hold a slightly overweight old man, but it might be nice to go out on the lake. Yah, I'll be glad to come if you think I can help. Ellie will be gone anyway—she's going down to spend some time in the Cities with our daughter—so yah, I'd like that. Like, just come back after the funeral and go to your place?"

"Right. I'll be there too, of course, so you can just follow me back. I really think I need your help on this. I'm beginning to wonder if I was ever cut out to be a sheriff after all."

Palmer recognized his window for evangelizing. "Don't say that, Jason. I'm sure you're doing a fine job. Just do the absolute best you can and do it with dignity. Let your light shine among others that, er, you know, um, they will see that you are in charge and are doing a, you know, good job."

Jason sounded puzzled as he said, "Yes, well, thanks. I'll do my best. Great! I'll see you Wednesday at the funeral then. Goodbye."

"Goodbye, Jason," said Knutson, and hung up the telephone with a look of worry and concentration. "Hmmm, I wonder who is up there that will speak only to me?" And what does he have to say?"

Chapter Eleven

Alan Sorgren stood in total detachment as his wife wrestled to open the heavy garage door. Carla Sorgren looked back at him sourly as she climbed into the driver's seat of their aging Pontiac. "I'm going to drive. I'm not sure you can handle it. Well, you coming or not?"

Alan Sorgren, sheriff of Monroe County, nodded and got in. He was thinking of the only subject that had occupied his mind for the past five days. He really needed a little bit of meth to get him through the day. As he stared with unseeing eyes through the window at the verdant countryside surrounding him, his wife knew exactly what he was going through. "It is really for the best, you know. And you're doing so well. I still think you should have checked into the clinic on Monday. The sooner you start rehab the better off you will feel."

"Yes, I know you're right. I just didn't want it to be a public event. I mean, if I don't show up for this funeral, everyone will want to know why. This way I can slip away Sunday night and we can merely say it was a medical leave. I can't say I'm very proud of being addicted to methamphetamines, nor am I proud of the way I have neglected my duties. And I have to say, I'm so grateful to you. The way you've stood by me this week, well, I mean, you're so much stronger than I am. I appreciate it, and I love you for it."

Carla blushed and wiped a tear from her eye. Yes, it would be different now. Alan would get the help he needed. They could start over. And while he was in the clinic, she'd lose twenty pounds. She looked dolefully into the mirror and saw that she had added a little more gray to her once shimmering auburn hair. Well, that would be taken care of too. Alan was always so gruff, not necessarily mean, but inattentive and rude. His words had moved her deeply. She reached over and took his hand and said, "I love you, too, Alan, and this is something we will get through together. Remember, I know what you are going through,"

They were dressed in their funeral clothes, and they were on their way to Durham to pay their respects to a fellow sheriff. "Did you know him very well, Alan?" she asked.

Alan passed his hand over the balding spot on his head and said, "No, I didn't. I had only met him once before. I said more words to him last Friday night than I had ever said before. And you know, I didn't like him much. If he'd lived much longer, he told me that he'd either blab publicly about the meth or he would tell a few select people about it. Like I said after that storm, I got the impression that he was setting me up for blackmail. Not to speak ill of the dead, but I'm not sorry he's gone."

"Me neither. I thought he was a little creepy, if you want to know the truth. But we can make the scene and say all the right things and get out of there. Besides, it gets us out of the house, a change of scenery that can get you through one more day. Oh, Alan. I don't know what I'm going to say if I have to talk to that Harvey Green today. Just think of the way he ruined our lives!"

"No, Carla, I don't want to think about it. I want to think of the future. I want to think of tasting good food again. I want to live a healthy lifestyle and maybe even put on some weight. I want to think of watching a Twins game on television and know what is really going on. And with you to help me, I know that this time I can do it."

* *

Fɪꜰᴛʏ ᴍɪʟᴇꜱ ᴀᴡᴀʏ, a light green Saturn sped along between lush fields of wheat. Denise Erstead turned to her husband and said, "Do you think the children will be all right staying at home? Marty wasn't too happy to learn that he would have to baby sit his little brother and sister for the day."

"Ah, sure, they'll be fine," Ronnie Erstead reassured her. "It's not like we make Marty do a lot around the house. When I was his age, I was out hauling bales. I tell ya, slinging bales up on a hayrack is a lot harder than hanging around on a summer's day just babysitting in your own home. Yah, he bellyached when I told him, but he's a good kid, and we can trust him."

The conversation, banal as it was, reflected once again the contrary nature of the two participants. Ronnie Erstead, sheriff of Harrison County, would always be positive and content that this was the best of all possible worlds, while his wife was always envious of worlds that seemed so much better. "I still don't see why you thought you had to go to this funeral, to say nothing of dragging me along. You know you didn't even like the guy."

"Well, what was I to do?" Ronnie responded defensively. "Everybody else will be there. I'd never even met the guy before Friday night, so I don't think it's fair to say I didn't like him."

"All right, I'll put it another way. From our brief encounter with him then, did you like him?"

"Okay, I have to admit that I didn't find him too charming, but those were unusual circumstances. Maybe under different conditions, he might have been a decent guy."

The road was straight and dry, there wasn't another car in sight, and the sheriff was delighting in going twenty miles faster than the speed limit. It felt good, real good. A perpetual optimist can never imagine anything bad happening to him, and he drove in the manner that he had played line-backer for the Bison—hard, fast and glorious. He frequently looked back on those days, and sometimes compared them to the mundane realities of his current position. Twenty years ago he was a blonde, blue eyed Viking specimen, with a body sculpted by trainers. Now he was a blonde, blue eyed Viking with a body sculpted by Cheetos. He was just think-ing of a game against the University of North Dakota Sioux, the hated rivals, when his wife said, "I thought you said he was a bad man?"

"Huh?" Ronnie said, jolted from his reverie.

"As I recall, you said he was one of those who was will-ing to carve up responsibilities of small counties. You im-plied that he was ready to join with that unspeakable Harvey Green to realign local law enforcement, and if they did that, Wham, you would be out of a job! What would happen to your dreams of owning a boat then?"

Ronnie looked in his rearview mirror just to check if there was anyone around and said, "Yah, well, that might have been the case. Did you hear the way he and Green were talking the other night? It sounded to me like they thought it might be a done deal. But with Charbonneau out of the way, I doubt if Green's little scheme will go very far. I heard that the governor will be at the funeral. Ordinarily, Green would take the oppor-tunity to press forward some oily plan to save money. Save money, cut taxes—that's what that weasel governor would like to hear. But now, well, without his little ally, it's going to be harder for Green to make that happen."

Denise checked her hair in the visor mirror. Petite and blonde, she still liked to think of herself as cute, and a fu-neral gave her a chance to wear her little black dress. Nev-ertheless, she always found funerals to be so tedious. She looked over at Ronnie and said, "So, it was rather handy that somebody offed him then?"

Ronnie chuckled and said, "I suppose if you put it that way, sure, I think I can get along without him just fine. But that's another reason why I think we should show up at the funeral. Keep in mind our little grilling from last Saturday. Like it or not, we are murder suspects, and there'll be some people looking at us that way."

"Oh, Ronnie," Denise said, but at the same time, she couldn't help thinking about how she had awakened in the middle of that Friday night and discovered that her husband had left the room. He later said that he couldn't get to sleep and just took a walk, but it was something he had never done before. When she had asked if he had told that to the police, Ronnie had simply said that he had forgotten to mention it. She recalled her husband's enthusiasm for that boat, and she wondered.

Meanwhile, Ronnie was thinking, "When I got back from my little walk that night, I was out like a light. Nothing could have awakened me. I suppose it is possible that Denise got up and . . . no, that's absurd."

❉ ❉

BRAD NICHOLS HAD ALWAYS PREFERRED the prairie half of his county. Whenever he passed into the forest part he felt claustrophobic. Maybe it was pretty, with the occasional lakes, but, as the son of a farmer, he always tended to think of the land as worthless. As he drove his ridiculously huge Ford Explorer along the highway with his wife, Karen, by his side, his mood was turning as black as his suit. Karen didn't have a black dress, she had told Brad, "I'm not a little black dress kind of person." She settled on a severe suit that was much too warm for the occasion.

"Think that church will be air conditioned?" she asked the sheriff of Hayes County.

"Don't know. I've never even been to that town. But it's probably not a large church, and small churches have needs other than air conditioning. I mean they use it one morning a week for a couple of hours. With a short Minnesota summer one would think they could put their money to better use. But maybe some rich guy decided to give 'em a present. Who knows? I'll tell you this much, though, I don't plan to spend any more time there than absolutely necessary. If they decide to plant him then and there, well, I'm not going to stand out in the sun by the side of the grave."

Karen sucked in on her large upper teeth and said, "You didn't like him much, did you?"

Brad pretended to give it some thought as he combed his mustache with his fingernails. "Of course, I really didn't know him well . . ."

"Horse dung! Don't give me that. I could tell when he was talking on Friday night that you couldn't stand the skinny little twerp."

The sheriff remembered the moment well. He had immediately reacted when Charbonneau started talking about department finances and looked at him with knowing eyes. Did he really know about the little skimming game he had going? He was sure that Karen didn't even know, and if she didn't know, how could a young sheriff in an inconsequential county know. But if he did know, did he tell others? Green looked as though he were gloating the whole time. Did the two of them block his promotion?

Aloud he finally admitted, "All right. I guess I didn't like his attitude."

"So how come we have to trundle our buns all the way up there for his funeral?"

"You didn't have to come along. I told you that. You could have said one of the boys was sick or something."

"At the time, it seemed like a good idea, going through the woods on a hot summer day and all that, but now . . . How come you think you have to go?

Brad shifted in his seat and said, "First of all, there's a certain solidarity among law enforcement professionals. Ever seen television reports of the big deals they make of a policeman or a fireman getting himself killed in New York or Chicago? Well, same here. Ya just feel like ya should go! And, I'd be lying if I didn't consider that there might be some bigger departments there and maybe I can keep my eye out for another job. And finally, you know, judging from those interrogations that we had to suffer through last Saturday, um, we're murder suspects, you know. How would it look if we didn't show up?"

"Oh, for heaven's sake. Nobody thinks that!"

"Don't they? Then who do you think they suspect, Palmer or Ellie Knutson? Maybe they were in it together."

Karen smiled, but looked deep into Brad's eyes. Clearly there was something he was not telling her.

* *

BEFITTING THE OCCASION, HARVEY GREEN decided to forgo the use of the county sheriff's vehicle and actually spend money for his own gas. He squeezed his pudgy form behind the wheel of his Cadillac, fiddled with the radio dial until he found a country music station, and cruised through his hometown like a liege lord overlooking his manor and all the peasantry within.

The sheriff of Green County tended to like funerals, now that more and more of his contemporaries were picking poppies from the root end. It gave him a certain satisfaction to know that he had outlasted them, especially those that had adopted a 'holier than thou' life style. He stuck a Marlboro in his face and rolled up the window so that the precious smoke did not escape with only one respiratory cycle.

Little Kevin Charbonneau didn't make it too long, did he, he chuckled to himself. *I doubt if he was even as old as his old man was when he bought the farm. It just seems that something happens to those who oppose the Green family. But what a way to go!* Green cast his mind back to the morning after the murder when he had carelessly crossed the yellow tape perimeter set up by the Bemidji police and generally mucked up the crime scene. Those cops were touchy. All in all, it was a particularly repulsive scene. There was still so much blood on the pavement by the statue that the chalk marks couldn't even stick properly.

No, he wheezed to himself as he rolled down the window to throw out the burning cigarette butt, *I'm not going to miss him at all. On the other hand, most people do not think it is a good idea to see sheriffs getting butchered. Maybe I can talk to the governor, give him the old "importance of our law enforcement officers in protecting the people" talk and remind him of his pledge to increase our funding. That would be fun, especially considering his big budget cut package. "Where's it going to come from then?" I'll ask, and watch him squirm. Or maybe not. It is a funeral, after all. Still, it wouldn't hurt to get him alone for a bit and remind him of the generous financial support he gets from the Grunwald Pines Resort. Yes, sir, the greatest governor money can buy!*

* *

PALMER KNUTSON PARKED HIS ACURA at the end of the parking row and walked to the church. There was something about Catholic churches that always made him nervous. Maybe it was the statuary. Maybe it was the fact that the interiors always seemed to be dark. On the other hand, the interior of the First Norwegian Lutheran Church in Fergus Falls was kind of dark too, when compared to the bright airiness of his little white country church. Maybe it was the smell. It was different, and Palmer suspected that it was the incense. Maybe it was the bowl of holy water that Palmer always tried to avoid. Or maybe it was the whole Mary thing or the confessional. Whatever it was, Palmer wasn't comfortable. As he walked up the aisle, he saw the coffin containing the mortal remains of the late Kevin Charbonneau, and he realized that he didn't feel properly bereaved. He found a seat and looked around him.

He noticed Ronnie and Denise Erstead come in, and watched them take a seat next to Brad and Karen Nichols. Over to the side he noticed Alan and Carla Sorgren, and couldn't help but think that Alan didn't look quite the ticket. In a pew near the front, Harvey Green sat, turning every fifteen seconds to look at the door. *Of course,* Palmer thought, *he's looking for the governor!* Sure enough, a few seconds later the governor came in with his entourage, and looked desperately for a pew other than the one already occupied by the sheriff of Green County. *Hail, hail, the gang's all here,* Knutson thought.

All of us who watched the storm, with the exception of Ellie, are here, Knutson said to himself, *and one of us may have sliced him up with a carving knife. But who? And why? None of them, er, us, I suppose, look particularly guilty.* Although Palmer attempted to follow along with the service, his eyes kept observing those people who had been with him in the Radisson ballroom only one week earlier.

The service was appropriate and mercifully short. The inconsolable widow induced feelings of pity and empathy. The music was appropriate and before long Kevin Charbonneau was offered into the arms of the Redeemer. Most, but not all, of those at the funeral followed the pallbearers and the casket out to a freshly dug grave. The priest said the usual sober words, then the widow, other family members, and close friends tossed handfuls of dirt on the coffin. Palmer could not help but observe the small group of people who had been with Charbonneau during his final hours. Brad and Karen Nichols had not accompanied the body to the grave, Palmer noticed, but the rest were there, none of them showing much sorrow. Out of the corner of his eye Palmer noticed that Harvey Green had come up to Alan Sorgren, clasped him warmly and led him a few steps away from his wife. Knutson noticed the extreme hostility in the eyes of Carla Sorgren and he noticed, as she didn't, the smile on the face of Harvey Green as he slipped something into the pocket of Alan's suit coat. He also thought he noticed an expression of relief on Alan's face.

CHAPTER TWELVE

PALMER WASN'T QUITE SURE HOW he had let himself get talked into it. The drive from the funeral was uneventful, except for the time when the governor's car sped past going at least ten miles over the speed limit. Palmer had been tempted to give him the finger, but Scandinavian politeness, the shame of acting like a juvenile, and the governor's reputation for retribution deferred his hand. He did notice, however, that Jason Two Bears, in the car ahead of him, did start to raise his hand.

He followed the acting sheriff of Beltrami County to his modest home on the lake. For some reason, Jason seemed to think the first thing to do was to take the boat out for a spin and then the talk turned to water skiing and then Palmer admitted that he used to like to water ski and the next thing he knew Palmer was in the water, overcoming his natural fear, and yelling, "Hit it!" He was soon terrifyingly aware that he was being pulled through the wake, with water forcing its way into his lungs. Belatedly he realized that he could just let go and he allowed his life vest to bob him to the surface. Well, he wasn't going to quit after only one try. Two more attempts, and two more gallons of water swallowed, and he was up. He glided along the surface of the water at what seemed to be one hundred miles an hour. After a few hundred yards he remembered how he used to "jump the wake" and he gave it a shot. It was perfect! He moved his skis to the outside arc and picked up speed and then came back and jumped to the other side. By this time his legs felt like two quivering cubes of Jell-O. He waved to

Jason and the boat brought him back to the dock. He held his balance until the final seconds and then splashed head-first and created a plume of water as though a piano had been dropped from a thousand feet.

Now he was sitting on a folding chair on the dock. His limbs were shaky. He was sore in every muscle of his body. He was sure that the water level of the lake must be down at least an inch from all the water he had swallowed, and he pictured minnows and assorted lake bacteria cohabiting his belly. His eyes smarted. And he felt absolutely wonderful!

Jason brought him a bottle of beer. "I thought a championship skier should be rewarded!"

"A Beck's! That's what I call a trophy! Give a guy a top job and he starts buying imported German beer."

"Actually, my favorite brand depends on what's on sale. But I noticed that you liked it last week, so I thought it was time to play host."

"Well," Palmer said. "You wouldn't have needed to do that. Your favorite beer sounds like my favorite. I like to keep it under fifty cents a can. But, I must admit, this is grand stuff. At least it doesn't taste like it has been passed through a Clydesdale!"

The two sheriffs told each other all they knew on the subject of beer, a procedure that really did not take up much time. Palmer looked across the edge of the lake and saw Lin Two Bears setting up a grill. He had high hopes for supper. Meanwhile, he said, "You know, I have never met your wife before. Is she, er, Native American too?"

Jason smiled. Under some circumstances, he would have considered the question to be rude and would have said so. But he knew Palmer genuinely cared. "No," he said. "She's Norwegian and Vietnamese. I'm part Irish, you know, so we might have some really interesting kids. Her father got drafted and was sent to Vietnam. He fell in love and brought a wife home with him. Something that didn't happen all that often in his northern Minnesota town! Interesting look, isn't it?"

"She is absolutely beautiful," Palmer said sincerely.

"So how come she married me, you wonder? The lord works in wondrous ways."

Palmer smiled and said, "Boy, does he ever!" He took another swig of beer and chuckled.

"I'm sure it caused somewhat of a stir when it happened, thirty years ago now," Jason mused. "People just weren't ready for that kind of thing."

Palmer rearranged his bathing suit for more comfort and said, "I guess you're right, but some of us were. In one sense, that could have been the most long lasting contribution my generation made. I don't know, maybe you don't agree. I should talk, I suppose, I'm a Norwegian male in one of the most heavily Norwegian areas of America. Talk about fitting in to the dominant culture. I guess what I'm trying to ask is, do you still feel prejudice on a daily basis?"

"That's a good question, and I guess I'd have to say no. I don't feel it on a regular basis as far as my personal life is concerned. But I probably do in the sense that it is hard to pick up a newspaper or listen to television without being saddened. For the most part, it isn't mean spirited, it is just ignorance. But even that is getting better, I think. And I'd have to give a lot of credit to guys like George Mitchell, Dennis Banks, and Clyde Bellecort. Back in the late sixties, they studied the old treaties, and attempted to define what 'sovereignty' meant to us. That was the start of AIM, the American Indian Movement, and out of that came some of the things you can find down in Minneapolis such as the Heart of the Earth Survival School, the Indian Health Board, and housing programs.

"But that wasn't easy, and they did some things that probably did more harm than good, such as the occupation of Wounded Knee in South Dakota in 1973. But even that, with the arrest and, as we would say, persecution, of Jerry Peltier, it did get a lot of attention. But you know, the more we looked into 'sovereignty,' the more we became aware of the treaties, like the treaty of 1837. Do you know about that one?

"I'm embarrassed to say that I don't," Palmer admitted.

"Don't be. Hardly anybody remembers it, unless you are a gung-ho sportsman, that is. You remember the old Vikings coach getting press for opposing fishing rights on Mille Lacs?"

"Yeah, now that you mention it."

"Well, that was enforcement of the treaty of 1837. Several bands of Ojibwe—including, I suppose, some of my ancestors—ceded the northern third of Wisconsin and most of northeast Minnesota to the United States Government in exchange for hunting, fishing and gathering rights and twenty years of annuity payments. What it did, of course, was to allow the lumber companies to come in and destroy our traditional environment. The way the U.S. government saw it at the time was that we were a sovereign nation. If so, doesn't that bind a nation to keep its treaties?

Palmer meekly said, "I suppose it does."

"In some ways, we got off easy compared to the Dakota tribes. Their big debacle was the Treaty of Travis Des Sioux in 1851."

Palmer brightened, "Now that I have heard of."

"And why not? It was one of the great land swindles of all time. After that treaty the United States government took all but four percent of the Dakota lands in Minnesota territory. Now traditionally, the Dakota had been our enemy, or so they say, and we actually started calling them 'Sioux,' which means 'snake in the grass.' Clearly a case of divided we fell. And you know what happened next, I suppose—the Great Sioux Uprising. 'Uprising!' That's what all the history books used to call it. The Dakota were cheated and starving and pushed beyond endurance. Apparently, it involved only a few young hotheads at first, but it spread rapidly. Some call it the largest of the American Indian Wars. Next to that, Custer and the Little Big Horn was chickenfeed. Hundreds of people were killed, farms abandoned, and all that nasty stuff. It didn't last too long, and Henry Hastings Sibley, fresh from serving as the first Minnesota governor, defeated Little Crow and the Dakota. Over three hundred of them were forced to stand trial for murder. The trials usually took no more than fifteen minutes each, and most of them were sentenced to hang."

Palmer interrupted by saying, "Yah, I know this part. Lincoln commuted the sentences for all but thirty-eight of 'em, but on Christmas Day they were all placed on this huge scaffold so that the trapdoors fell at the same time and all of 'em were hanged at the same instant. I remember it because of my imagination of the horror of that scene, which apparently was witnessed by hundreds of people. Barbaric! It was the largest mass execution in American history."

Jason Two Bears sighed and said, "Yes, but I have to keep reminding myself that is was a different time involving different people. It was in the midst of the Civil War, and I suppose people were already starting to become brutalized."

"I know," Palmer said, "but it just seems like such a collective guilt for the people of Minnesota. I suppose, in one way, I could say that my ancestors had nothing to do with it. They were still dirt-poor farmers in Norway at the time, but other Norwegians, and Swedes, and Germans, and Yankees were here, and in the long run we were all able to take advantage ot the removal of the Indians."

Jason smiled. "You hear what you're saying? Some of my friends consider expressions such as that to be nothing more than trite conscience-salving. But I don't. I see it as a way to permanent reconciliation. They have this plaque that they set up in Mankato, on the exact site of where those thirty-eight men were hanged. It contains a prayer written by Amos Owen, a Dakota spiritual leader. I was so moved that—although I don't remember trying to—I memorized it. It goes, "Grandfather, I come to you this day in a humble way to offer prayers for the thirty-eight Dakota who perished in Mankato in the year 1862. To the West, I pray to the Horse Nation and to the North, I pray to the Elk People. To the East, I pray to the Buffalo Nation, and to the South, the Spirit People. To the Heavens, I pray to the Great Spirit and to the Spotted Eagle. And Below, I pray to Mother Earth to help us in his time of reconciliation. Grandfather, I offer these prayers in my humble way. To all my relations."

Palmer heard the words pronounced in the flat cadence of the Native American peoples. It seemed as though more than one county sheriff was talking, as the words seemed to roar from a thousand ancestors. The late afternoon sun danced off the waters of Lake Bemidji and momentarily blinded him. At the last word, a silence of unbearable intensity existed between the two men. Finally, Palmer managed to gasp out, "Thank you. Thank you for telling me."

Men sometimes get embarrassed at such intense moments, and after a couple of seconds, Jason said, "Yeah, well, that's not what I brought you up here for. You are supposed to help me solve a crime. But not," he added just as Palmer started to open his mouth, "before we've had a couple of steaks. You like 'em rare?

Palmer smiled and said, "Just barely warm," and stood up. His bathing suit was mostly dry, but was still wet in the uncomfortable areas. He had been sitting in the sun for forty minutes and his skin, previously a uniform snowy white, had begun to look as though he had bathed in tomato juice. "Do you suppose we would have time for another beer after I've changed?"

"Absolutely!" Jason reassured him.

CHAPTER THIRTEEN

FTER SUPPER PALMER SAID A SERIES of ostentatious "thank yous" to Lin Two Bears and gallantly offered to help with the dishes. She declined his offer, as Palmer was profoundly hoping she would. With coffee and a plate of brownies set between them, Knutson and Two Bears sat in the screened in porch and listened to the music of the loons. Finally, Palmer said, "So, what can I do to help on this Charbonneau case?"

Jason sipped his coffee and said, "I'm not sure you can really do anything. I've gone over the transcripts of all the interviews we conducted on Saturday, and, with Neil Meyer's help, I've collected a lot of information, but . . ."

"Neil Meyer?" Palmer interrupted, "When did you talk to him? How's he doing?"

"He seems happy as a clam, catching all the fish he ever dreamed of, apparently. I tracked him down and gave him a call on Sunday morning. There were enough loose threads to be found in the testimonies we took on Saturday morning that just had to be followed up. He gave me several ideas on who to contact and where I could go to find out more information. I just thought that you, since you've been county sheriff since God was a boy, well, you might be in a unique position to help me sort out some of this."

Palmer scowled. "I admit that I've been around for a while, but why would I have any particular insight into any of them?"

Jason picked up a sheaf of papers and said, "I have here the transcripts of eight people, including Ronnie Erstead,

Denise Erstead, Alan Sorgren, Carla Sorgren, Brad Nichols, Karen Nichols, Harvey Green, and one Palmer Knutson."

Palmer did not immediately notice the obvious omission.

"Now, you can read all of these, and I urge you to do so, because it's likely that I missed something, but they all tell the same story. They are all, in fact, remarkably similar to the testimony that you gave. There is the same general reporting of the storm, a general description of where people sat, and a mention of the wine—with overwhelming approval, I might add. All say that there was a lot of tension in the room, but none could identify this with anything said or actions taken. Everybody mentions discussions of past tornadoes, including a tedious and meandering account of every storm Harvey Green ever saw. They all agree that your wife first spotted the tornado, that it hailed violently but for only a short time, and that the lights did go out for less than a minute. Allowing for possible exaggerations by Green, I have no reason to believe that anything recorded in those interviews is not the gospel truth. In other words, assuming that you told the gospel truth, they all agreed with you and added nothing substantially to the recollected events of that night."

Palmer shrugged and said, "Yah, if you want me to review these, I can do that, although I don't see much hope of gaining new information."

Jason shifted through the transcripts and handed him a copy of the testimony of the Sheriff of Otter Tail County. "Here," he said. "Read yours first. Then read the others and see if you can spot inconsistencies and see if you can make any judgments on them."

Palmer fished out his reading glasses and began to read the words he had spoken only five days earlier. As he read, Palmer became quite pleased with himself. *Now this*, he thought, *is a fine account of what happened that night. Nothing left out, nothing inconsequential. If only all witnesses were capable of this.*

When he finished, Jason said, "Do you have anything to add to that?"

Palmer shrugged his shoulders and said, "Nothing that occurs to me right now."

"All right, read the others and see what you think."

One by one Palmer read the transcriptions of the interviews with Ronnie Erstead, Denise Erstead, Alan Sorgren, Carla Sorgren, Harvey Green, Karen Nichols, and Brad Nichols. For the most part, he was impressed. *Each of the transcripts are almost as good as my testimony,* he thought and he could find no obvious omissions or additions. When he was finished, and Jason had refilled his coffee cup, he handed them to the Beltrami County Acting Sheriff and said, "Yah, well, collectively that seems to sum it all up, I guess. I certainly can't see any motive for murder there."

Jason looked at him rather intensely and said, "What would you say if I could identify a motive for murder for each one of them?"

"My first reaction would be that you are one highly imaginative sheriff. But then I would naturally ask you to tell me just what you mean."

Jason took a deep breath and replied, "All right, here it goes. Ronnie Erstead seems to be about as honest as the Statue of Liberty, and about as imaginative. I could find no hint of any kind of malfeasance there, with the possible exception of the personal use of a lot of county equipment and resources. How do I know this? Well, it seems good old Neil has a nephew that owns the Thrivent Insurance agency in Grimstead. It seems that he and Erstead have a fairly regular meeting for morning coffee, and Neil told me to use his name to see what I could find out. I called up the nephew and told him about the award that you were given and, er, while never actually saying so, I let him think that Erstead, you know, might be in line for it next year. Anyhow, the guy gets to talking and I can't shut him up. According to him, Erstead has been worried constantly about a rather vague attempt to reorganize functions of county sheriffs. Hardly anybody lives in Harrison County anymore, you know, and there have been suggestions that some of the duties of county sheriffs could be consolidated into some sort of regional law enforcement arrangement. Ergo, Erstead, who apparently has no ambition to be anything but the sheriff of Harrison County, would be out of a job. Neil's nephew said, and I paraphrase, but you get the idea, "he told me that he knew that some guy named Green was behind it, but that he was backed up by some other weasel, even though he didn't know who. It seems that Erstead was once a pretty tough football player, and the nephew said that the only time he saw that side of potential violence was when he was talking about that guy. Of course, he was telling me this in a 'good old Ronnie Erstead' way of talking, almost like he admired him for latent violence. The only other thing, besides the shared county resources issue, is apparently a running joke all over town ever since a birthday party for one of Erstead's kids featured 'Harrison County Sheriff's Department' napkins." Palmer sat listening with a fresh beer.

"Now if, and clearly this is only speculation, Erstead found out who was organizing an attempt to have his job cut out from under him, would he be capable of solving the problem with a carving knife? Who knows? I also asked Neil's nephew about Denise Erstead. This was kind of interesting, in that he had the impression it was Mrs. Erstead who had the pants of ambition in the family. Would she act if her husband did not? Could she have taken the knife and carved up Charbonneau because he was one of the people who threatened her livelihood? Stranger things have happened."

"Yah, but still," Palmer began, then remembered recent murder cases of his own. "All right, what else did you find out?"

Jason put on a pained expression and said, "The story of Alan Sorgren is kind of sad. Neil knew his predecessor, who still lived in the county. He said that if anyone would know what was going on there, he would. So I called him up. He didn't want to talk at all, implying that to do so was a betrayal of a man he still respected. Well, I had to say how much I admired his loyalty and tried to butter him up and play the Neil Meyer card harder than ever, but I finally got him to open up. He says Alan Sorgren has an addiction problem. Sorgren confided that to him a few months ago, and told him that he had gone cold turkey and was off methamphetamines. Sorgren was most anxious that the story of his addiction, which he indicated was caused by another sheriff, should never be revealed. This was the only time the two ever spoke about it, but apparently Sorgren was filled with loathing for the man who had gotten him hooked. The old sheriff was supportive, or so he told me, but he was more worried that Sorgren had never really kicked the habit."

"Wow, Palmer said. "Did you find anything out about his wife?"

"Yes, unfortunately. It seems that for a while she was even a more enthusiastic user of meth than he was. She, fortunately, was able to kick the habit—had a hell of a time doing it, according to the old sheriff. She's a rather large woman who looks like she could handle herself, and somebody else, if it comes to that. It does not take a leap of imagination to see her slicing up the guy who is virtually poisoning her husband."

Palmer nodded, "Yah, I can see her doing that physically. I don't know her well enough to be able to say she is psychologically capable, however."

"The old sheriff said she would protect Alan like a mother bear protects her cubs," Jason added.

"But surely," Palmer said, "not Brad or Karen Nichols."

"Well, I know this is going to disappoint you, but there could be something there, too. This is really under the table stuff. According to Neil, a county commissioner is currently conducting an extremely covert investigation of the expenditure of funds in the Sheriff's Office. Neil told me that Brad Nichols has been bitter about his job ever since he was torpedoed in his attempt to move up to a better job in suburban Minneapolis."

Palmer nodded and said, "Yah, I remember that. He's complained to me several times about it. And now that I think about it, he is not the cheerful guy he used to be. But stealing?"

"Neil didn't really think there was anything to it. It seems it has something to do with emergency disaster funds and are not what they should be, and rumors that Nichols is living beyond his means."

Palmer said, "That's ridiculous. You could skim off a few hundred bucks here and there if you put your mind to it, but it would hardly be enough to change your life style. I can see Brad "borrowing" from one fund to pay another, he's been at that job for quite a while, but he would know that could never go undetected for long, and it just wouldn't be worth it. But the anger about losing that job, the chance to move up, now that might be something!"

"That's what I was thinking," Jason said. "And according to Neil, he had been quite vocal about his suspicions that he was torpedoed by a fellow sheriff. Apparently, Meyer heard him virtually accusing Harvey Green of badmouthing him, and said that he was sure that at least one other sheriff was behind it. Revenge? An age-old motive! And Karen Nichols? It might be more than a 'stand by your man' kind of thing. She was more eager to get out of Northwest Minnesota and seek the bright lights of the city than he was. And now it appears they will be stuck there for the rest of their lives. Oh, yeah, she could handle a blade with the best of them if she had to."

Palmer grimaced and said, "Ouch, you could be right! And I already know about Harvey Green, but I would have thought more people would have a motive to murder him than the other way around."

"Just a minute, Palmer. Didn't you notice that someone's account of what happened that night was not included?" Two Bears added quickly.

"No, it seemed like you mentioned everyone who was there, didn't you?"

"What about your wife, Palmer? What about Ellie?"

"Oh, yah. I thought you interviewed her, too. So where's her transcript?"

Two Bears smiled and said, "Right here, Palmer. And I must say it is one of the most remarkable masterpieces of observation I have ever run across. I'd like you to read this, and see if this account provides us with a better understanding of what went on that night."

Palmer blinked, took the manuscript, and started reading.

Lt. Jack Hanson:

"The subject of this interview is Ellie Knutson. The place is the Radisson Hotel in Bemidji, Minnesota, and the time is 10:32 a.m. The subject has been informed of her rights and has agreed to the recording of this interview. Now, Mrs. Knutson, will you inform us of the circumstances under which you were gathered in the ballroom of the Radisson Hotel between 7:00 and 8:30 yesterday evening?

Ellie Knutson:

"Yes. I was attending a banquet for the Northwestern Minnesota Association of County Sheriffs. My husband,

Palmer Knutson, was to give the keynote address. It was a responsibility he took very seriously and, having heard it a few times, I can assure you that it was a very good speech."

J.H:

"But he didn't give the entire speech, did he, Mrs. Knutson. Will you tell us what happened?

E.K:

"Yes. It turned out to be less of a formal speech than a surprise party. Unbeknownst to my husband, the other members of the Association had decided to honor him for his years of service. His deputy, Orly Peterson, got up and gave a very nice speech. There was the usual clapping and good-natured fellowship one always finds during such an occasion, and a plaque was awarded to my husband. Unfortunately, Palmer still felt obligated to give his speech." Palmer winced as he read these words.

Sheriff Jason Two Bears:

"And then what happened?"

E.K:

"Someone from the hotel staff rushed in to tell everyone that we were under a tornado warning. Everybody jumped up like their pants were on fire. I've never seen anything like it. I think Palmer would really have liked to bathe in the glow of the honor—he is a very humble man, but I could tell that the award pleased him a great deal—but suddenly there was no time. Orly Peterson and his new bride, who were seated next to us, jumped up and were gone with hardly a 'by your leave.' For a time, there was a short line of people wanting to shake Palmer's hand, but the rest of the people streaked for the exit. The servers seemed to vanish into thin air. In no time at all there were just a few of us left in the room."

J.H:

"And what happened next?

"We moved from a rather awkward arrangement, one that had Palmer and me sitting at a large rectangular head table with the others scattered across the room, over to a more congenial setting. This was my husband's suggestion, since it gave us a perfect and, I must say, dramatic view of the storm. We gathered around three round tables next to the large windows on the west side of the ballroom. The three tables were close together to facilitate conversation and the sharing of wine, which Palmer brought over from the open bar. I meant to ask him if anybody was ever going to pay for that wine, but I haven't had a chance to ask yet."

J.T:

"That's all right, Mrs. Knutson, I'll take care of it. Go on."

Palmer looked up at his host, and a blush would have been discernable were it not for the sunburn.

E.K:

"Good. Well, as Palmer said, we were in a perfect spot to watch the storm come in. My husband has always been fascinated by thunderstorms, and from the timbre of the conversation, it would seem that many of the others were, too. In any event, none of them seemed in a hurry to scurry off, and we sat there in rather peaceful contemplation of the exciting weather just outside the windows."

J.T:

"Would you share the gist of that conversation with us?"

E.K:

"Certainly. At first, most of the talk was about the experience that the various contributors had with previous storms. In retrospect, the conversation seemed to be dominated by the males of the group. I don't know if tornados are like football and firecrackers—that is, women usually have better things to talk about—or whether the women just lacked experience in that area. To a certain extent, it got to be a little bit of a contest. Who had the most outrageous tornado story to tell? It got a little ridiculous when Harvey Green started his exaggerations, I mean, he claimed a tornado had picked a swimming pool up out of the ground!"

J.H:

"Can you describe the atmosphere at the time?"

E.K:

"What? Well, it was, oh, you mean of the conversation, I thought you meant outside. We didn't have the windows open, of course, so I'm not sure of that, but it certainly looked threatening. But inside, it seemed cordial enough to start with, but it soon got very chilly. It seemed like the real instigator of things was that Charbonneau. He had a habit of saying something that seemed on the surface to be innocent enough, but then he would stare at one or another person with a kind of gloating, or self-satisfaction, or, oh, I don't know, but enough so that the person blushed, or looked away, or returned a look of genuine hatred. I would guess everyone in the room was aware of that."

In reading this, Palmer looked at Jason Two Bears and gave him an apologetic shrug.

J.T:

"Do you recall which statements by Charbonneau caused the most discomfort?"

E.K:

"I'll try. Let's see. I think I first noticed it when he started talking about a methamphetamine laboratory that had been destroyed by a storm in his county. While he was saying this, he never took his eyes off of Alan Sorgren. It seemed at the time to be a rather uninteresting story, I mean, the meth lab was in a trailer house, and those things get hit by tornados all the time, but I just couldn't help noticing how Sorgren reacted. He was already looking jumpy when the storm started, but now it was worse. In fact, it occurred to me that maybe he was on something. You can never tell these days. Anyway, then I looked over at his wife, what's her name, Carla? And she had a look on her face that was a cross between fury and fear. I remember thinking at the time that maybe it might be some phobia about storms—we had a dog once that just went nuts during a thunderstorm—but in retrospect, it was something else. She shot daggers at Charbonneau for a bit, and then she looked with fear at her husband. After a bit, Sorgren looked away and I saw Charbonneau look over at Harvey Green, and they seemed to share some kind of satisfied smirk. Carla Sorgren noticed that and gave Green a look that would have made Medusa's gaze seem positively benevolent. There was much more there than the storm!"

J.H:

"Was this the only personal conversation that went on during this time?"

E.K:

"No. Far from it. Harvey Green seemed to feel that he could be every bit as nasty as Charbonneau, and pretty soon it was apparent that he had chosen Ronnie Erstead as his victim. It seemed as though he was baiting him because he was the sheriff of a small, under-populated county and didn't have much work to do. He implied that the way forward, was to consolidate some of the sheriff's duties with other counties. In other words, he was clearly questioning Erstead's position and his usefulness to society. I thought it was petty and mean, and I noticed Ronnie's wife sitting there with clenched fists. When he had finished his little needling of Erstead, he looked over at Chabonneau as if to say, 'How do you like them apples? I can make 'em squirm too. 'What a nasty creature!"

J.H:

"What were the other people doing while this part of the discussion proceeded?"

E.K:

"I'm not sure I can answer that. The interchange was so intense that I tended to just look at the persons involved. Besides, you know, the weather was getting very interesting at about that time, and everybody had one eye on the window. I do remember that no sooner had Green finished baiting poor Ronnie Erstead than Charbonneau seemed eager to change the subject and talk about funding for disaster relief. At the time, I thought is was a wise thing to do, and given what could just happen to the city of Bemidji at any minute, an apropos subject."

J.T:

"What did he say, Mrs. Knutson."

E.K:

"I thought at first that it was a perfectly legitimate topic. He merely started talking about how it was necessary to have a reserve fund in place to take care of those emergencies that are never supposed to happen but do. He made a nice comparison to the way that F.E.M.A. had responded in Grand Forks to the way it had responded to the disaster of Hurricane Katrina. But then, it seemed, he got a little personal. He looked Brad Nichols in the eye and said something about how he had heard of sheriffs who used a disaster fund as their own personal piggy bank. The implication was clear. He as much as accused Nichols of skimming funds. I expected Brad to stand up and slug him. Instead, Brad turned white as a sheet. Just then lightening struck very nearby and his face looked positively grotesque. I looked back at Charbonneau and he had a look on his face that could only be described as triumphant. He turned his grin to Green as much as to say "right back at you, Harvey.""

J.T:

"How did Green react to that?"

E.K:

"For a moment they just looked at each other as if in admiration. It was just bizarre. I mean, lighting is flashing, thunder rolling, the storm was just about upon us . . . then Charbonneau looked directly at Green and said something like, 'it's one thing to keep track of funds, but keeping track of prisoners is something else, isn't it Harvey?' Wow! I mean, if it would have been the old west I think Green would have gone for his gun!"

J.T:

"And then?'

E.K:

"Then I happened to spot the tornado. I yelled and pointed it out and everybody rushed to the window. To tell you the truth, I totally forgot about that whole conversation until you brought it up. I mean, it is quite exciting looking at a funnel cloud at close range, wondering if it is going to touch down and take you to the land of Oz!"

J.H:

"I imagine so. Tell me, at any time did you see anyone near the carving cart?"

E.K:

(Hesitation)

"Yes and no. That is, I'm not sure. Almost as soon as the funnel cloud suddenly disappeared, a tremendous gust of wind hit the hotel. For about, oh, I don't know, maybe forty to forty-five seconds, we lost electricity. The lightning was almost constant, so it was like a strobe light. I have a vague feeling of people moving around, getting away from the windows, and, as I recall the carving cart wasn't far away. I just have a feeling, with no real certainty and absolutely no ability to identify anyone, that someone was in that area. I'm sorry I can't tell you more."

J.T:

"And when the lights came back on?"

E.K:

"You know what it was like? It was like when the movie ends and they turn the lights. Like 'It's over, time to go home.' The hail really didn't last much longer. The wind dropped way down. The danger of a tornado seemed to be over. It was as though someone had banged a gavel and said 'meeting adjourned.' We just left the room, and I can't even recall anything other than expressions of relief we had survived. I'm sorry, but that's really all I can tell you."

D.K:

"Thank you, Mrs. Knutson. You have been a most informative witness to that night and we appreciate your observations."

E.K:

"You're most welcome, and don't hesitate to call me if I can be of any further help"

J.T:

"I have to admit, Mrs. Knutson, you are probably the best witness I have ever . . ."

(End of tape)

Palmer put down the transcript and looked up proudly at Jason. "Well, she certainly acquitted herself well. Especially next to my pathetic statement! And I'm supposed to be the professional."

Jason looked at Palmer with a quizzical expression. "Didn't the two of you talk about that night?

"Yah," Palmer said, "but I suppose she just figured that since I was there that I saw the same thing she did."

"Just curious, but do you talk about your cases with her?"

"Sometimes, sure. But she never talks about them with other people."

"Well," Jason said with admiration, "she sure is willing to talk with 'authorities.' Just a hell of an interview and provides more insight into this case than anything else, don't you think? Now, I'm going to ask you for you opinion of what might have happened in light of what you have just read. But first, I should tell you about something that we have not made public. Only those intimately concerned with the investigation know this. Charbonneau went to his death with a hunting knife in a sheath kept in the small of his back. In other words, he went to meet his killer fully armed. Okay, the ball is in your court, Palmer, what do you deduce from all of that?"

Knutson leaned back in his chair. Jason added more coffee to both cups, pulled out a small bottle of brandy and, receiving a nod of approval from his fellow sheriff, proceeded to add a generous shot. Knutson sipped in appreciation while collecting his thoughts and said, "All right, here's the way I see it. Both Green and Charbonneau know, or at least think they know, something about their fellow sheriffs. I feel like such a dolt. I sat there the whole time and just thought people were afraid of the storm. I never actually put how they were acting and what they were saying together. Now, to what end was this being done? Was it blackmail? Of what kind? Charbonneau was young, and maybe he thought he needed the money. Green has always had a streak of venality. But maybe it was just power. Some people get a kick out of holding a threat over other people. I didn't know Charbonneau all that well, but on reflection, I can see him doing it. Green? Sure, he loved to be ornery just to be ornery, if you know what I mean. So here these guys are having their own private pissing contest at the expense of everyone else until . . . what? According to Ellie's statement, Charbonneau dropped some kind of bombshell about the treatment of prisoners, or something like that, and then the tornado is spotted and the conversation doesn't go any further.

"Now, if Ellie's recollection is accurate, from the evidence of that transcript one would have to conclude that Green heard something from Charbonneau that shocked him. The implications of what Ellie discerned are a little discomforting. I mean, here are these sheriffs, some of whom I have known for years, who may or may not have done something for which they can be blackmailed. And it brings me to what I have always felt about this case. Now bear in mind that I don't know the wives of these men all that well, but it would seem to me that they would all have a similar motive, that is, to protect their husbands. Heaven knows that women are just as capable of murder as men, but for the time being, I'll leave them out. With your permission, I'll also exclude Ellie and myself as suspects. Charbonneau is excluded because he was the victim, of course, so that leaves four major suspects. Of those four, I can see any of them getting caught by circumstances or temptation to the point of doing something they shouldn't. But I can see only one who is possibly depraved enough to commit murder. I have not said anything before because it is only a gut feeling, but Ellie's testimony about how Charbonneau seemed to spit outa challenge in the last exchange before she spotted the tornado tends to confirm the way I've always felt about this. I think Harvey Green is the only one capable of committing the murder. Do you have any proof at all?"

Dismally Jason shook his head and said, "Not a shred. I really didn't know any of those guys, but from my opportunity to interview them, it seemed to me that most of them were essentially harmless. All except Harvey Green, but I just assumed I felt as I did because he has been such a racist pain in the ass all those years. But a lot of times, people like that are, fundamentally, cowards. A coward does not steal a knife and butcher somebody."

Palmer just shrugged and said, "Don't they? I think if the threat is great enough they are capable of anything. Anyway, for what it's worth, I'd have to say to concentrate your investigation on Green. What does he say he was doing at the time of the murder?"

Two Bears picked up the transcripts and turned to Green's. "Let's see . . . here it is . . . 'I was sleeping?' Asked if he had anyone to corroborate that statement—all right, I admit, I asked the question awkwardly—he said 'No such luck. One of the few times I've gone to a conference and have ended up sleeping alone.' In other words, no alibi."

Palmer nodded and contemplated his left thumb. "Oh," he exclaimed, "you still haven't told me, what is this about someone who will speak only to me? What is that all about? Who is it?"

"I assume it will have something to do with this case. He called me not long after the murder became public and said that he needed to talk to you about the murder. After you agreed to come up here, I called him back and he said that there was probably no hurry and that he would wait until you were here. I've made an appointment for us to see him at my office at ten o'clock tomorrow morning?"

"Hmm, who is he?"

"He is a technologist at the Bureau of Criminal Apprehension laboratory here in Bemidji. His name is Greg Refsdahl. Know any Refsahls?"

"The name sounds familiar. Oh, I know, the kid who took my older daughter to the senior prom was a Refsdahl. But I'm sure it's not him. Well, we'll find out tomorrow, I guess."

"Yeah, let's call it a night."

Chapter Fourteen

THURSDAY MORNING WAS OVERCAST AND HUMID. The lake didn't look quite so much like the land of sky blue waters. Knutson and Two Bears went to the office of the Beltrami County sheriff. Palmer noticed that they walked right by the office of Neil Meyer, where nothing had changed since Palmer had last been there. Jason led the way to his small, windowless room.

"I suppose you're going to move into Neil's office one of these days," Palmer said, viewing Two Bears' office with obvious distaste.

Jason plopped down on his rather precarious chair and answered, "Oh, one of these days, I suppose. But Meyer has to get his stuff out of there first. I don't need to press him on it. Besides, maybe after a couple of weeks of fishing he will change his mind."

The two sheriffs were there to meet Greg Refsahl, a meeting Knutson looked forward to with unrestrained curiosity. *"Why me?"* He thought.

Jason provided a cup of coffee that was, if anything, worse than what Palmer was used to in the Otter Tail County Law Enforcement Center. Naturally, he praised it, causing Two Bears to doubt either his sincerity or his taste. They waited in rather embarrassed silence until Jason's secretary leaned in and said, "Were you expecting a visitor? In any event, he's here."

Jason left the room and returned shortly with a tall thin man with a receding hairline, glasses, and a pen protector in his pocket. He appeared to be in his late twenties. Palmer squinted and said, "Yes. It is you. I remember your mother calling you 'Greggor McFeggor.' I believe you took Maj to the prom. How are you?"

"Um, er, I'm fine. Nobody, even my mother, has called me that in years. How's Maj? I guess I've sort of lost track of her. I mean, after graduation I know that she went off to Gustavus Adolphus College and I went down to the U. of M. I did see her at our five-year class reunion, and at the time she was in law school. How did that all work out?"

Palmer grinned proudly and said, "Fine, just fine. She's working as a lawyer in the Twin Cities, and she's married. And no, I'm not a grandfather yet. But what about you? What brings you to Bemidji?'

Refsahl swallowed and said, "Well, that's pretty much why I wanted to see you. As Mr. Two Bears here might have told you, I'm working as a technologist at the State Bureau of Criminal Apprehension laboratory here. I graduated from the University with a degree in pathology, specializing in DNA applications, and this is my first job. I've run across something, and done something, for which I need some personal advice. I wonder if Mr. Two Bears will excuse us for a few minutes?"

Palmer furrowed his brow and said, "I'm sure he will, but are you sure he should not be a part of this? I mean if it pertains to the murder, he is one of the major investigators. I'm sure you can rely on his discretion."

Refsahl shifted his feet uncomfortably and replied. "Yes. I'm sure I can. And I do want to talk to you both together. I would just like a word with you first, if you don't mind."

Jason stood and said, "Of course. You can just stay here. I've got a couple of other issues to attend to." He closed the door behind him as he left.

An interminable silence enveloped the two remaining occupants of the room. Finally, not being able to take it any more, Knutson said, "Well?"

With a deep sigh, Refsahl plunged in. "When we were growing up in Fergus Falls, we were all sort of in awe of you. I mean, it took up a lot of courage for me to ask the daughter of the sheriff to go to the prom with me. About all we knew ·of you was when we saw you in parades or when you came to the school to talk to our class. But believe me, you have always had a very high reputation in Fergus Falls, and I just thought I could trust you with what could be a tricky problem."

Palmer held up his hand and said, "All right, maybe I can help you, maybe I can't. But you must be warned that if you've done anything illegal I'll have to share that information. You may want to consult a lawyer, because I'm not qualified or capable of giving legal advice."

Refsahl rubbed his mouth and said, "Yes. I know. I guess what I need to know is whether or not I need legal council."

"Okay. As long as that is clear, I'll do what I can. What's the problem?"

Refsahl straightened in his chair and began, "So here's the deal. I often work long hours at the lab. Sometimes test results are not available immediately and I have to wait for them. Many nights I'm all alone in the lab. One night, about four weeks ago, the sheriff of Carson County, Kevin Charbonneau, the guy who got himself murdered last week, knocked at the door of the lab. I told him that the lab was closed, and he said that he was aware of that, and that was why he had come by when he did. He said he had a DNA test that he wanted me to run. I told him that wouldn't be a problem and that he should just come by during the daytime so we could do the proper paperwork. By this time, he had eased himself through the door and said that what he wanted done was so secret that he couldn't share it with anyone. He said he had two samples of tissue that he was sure contained DNA, and that all he wanted was to prove to himself, at least for the time being, that they were a match. He said he was working on a very sensitive case and it was imperative that no one find out about it until he had proceeded in his investigation." Refsahl took a breath, then continued.

"Well, what was I going to do? Even though we were about the same age, he was a county sheriff, and I was a mere pathologist. I'm the low man on the totem pole here anyway, and I figured, since I worked so many evenings as it was, that I could help him out and keep my mouth shut. He promised me that if the samples were not a match, well, then it would be better and no one would ever know, but if they were, it would be a real feather in both of our caps if a murder was solved. I guess it flattered me."

He paused and appeared to be distracted by the zipper of his trousers. Finally Palmer said, "Yes, all right, go on."

Looking Palmer in the eye, Refsahl said, "Science is a marvelous thing, you know, and we are making such strides. I was very lucky to have professors at the University who had access to all the latest developments. Do you know that forensic scientists need only one-billionth of a gram of material for DNA testing? DNA can be found on almost anything that comes in contact with a perpetrator. In this case, he handed me two small envelopes, each containing a single hair. There was ample follicular tissue on each. I told him that it would be quite simple to examine them for a match, and told him to come back in a week.

"So I did that. One of the envelopes was labeled 'crime scene' and the other was labeled with the name of 'Richard Stumpf.' It turned out to be an indisputable match. When he returned, I gave him the samples back and my report. He seemed extraordinarily pleased."

Palmer scratched his belly, where the sunburned skin was starting to itch, and said, "Yah, well, I can see where you have a right to be concerned. That kind of private investigation is clearly a breech of procedure. You must notify your superiors at the BCA if you haven't already done so, but I hardly think you're in any real trouble."

"Wait. There's more. When I gave him the report, he said, 'Here, this is for your troubles, and gave me a hundred dollars. I was overjoyed. I mean, I'm just starting out, and a hundred bucks a week before payday meant a lot. It was only after he had gone that I started to worry that if anybody found out about that I would really be in trouble."

"Hmm," Palmer said, "and you've told nobody about this?"

"Nope."

"Did he pay by check?"

"No. He slipped a hundred dollar bill in my shirt pocket. I thought that nobody would ever have to know and then I find out that Charbonneau was murdered. I did a little checking in the records. I mean, who was this Richard Stumpf? It turns out that he was once a prime suspect in a murder committed about twenty years ago, and that the victim was a guy called Charbonneau. He was not charged in the murder, however, because at the time he was locked up in the Green County jail. It was at this point that I called Mr. Two Bears."

Palmer thought for a minute and then said, "Okay, here's what we'll do. Let's keep our mouths shut about that hundred bucks. It's not like you can return it, and it certainly wouldn't do your career any good if it came out that you were moonlighting, using a state laboratory, for your own profit. I'm sure you'll never do anything like that again, and if your conscience bothers you, well, then, maybe some day when you can afford it, you can give it to some charity with interest. But it must forever remain something that is just between the two of us, understand?"

Refsahl made a long exhalation of breath and said, "Thank you, Mr. Knutson. I shall never forget this, but what do we do next."

Palmer put his sheriff face back on and said, "We call in Jason Two Bears and you repeat everything you told me on the record, leaving out the money, of course. When and if this case comes to trial, you'll be called to testify. Meanwhile, right after you leave here, you must give a complete account to your supervisors at the BCA, minus, of course, the money. I'll go and get the sheriff and recording equipment."

* *

After Refsahl gave his testimony, he was dismissed. Jason and Palmer sat looking at each other across the small room. "Well," said Two Bears.

"Exactly," said Knutson. "Are you thinking what I'm thinking?"

"What else? Green has this Stumpf locked in his jail. He lets him out to murder the only real competition to his family's resort business. Stumpf kills Charbonneau's father and comes back to jail. He has the perfect alibi. It is impossible for him to have committed the murder because he has been behind bars. He serves what little sentence he has left, more than likely gets a nice payment from the Green brothers, and leaves the state. Kevin Charbonneau makes it his life work to be the nemesis of Green, becomes a lawman, and uses every arrow in his quiver, if you don't mind the reference, to find the truth of his father's murder. He finds it. Now, look back at your wife's testimony, on the night of the storm, the very last conversation she recalls is an ominous reference to Green about keeping track of prisoners. He knows, and he lets Green know he knows. I think we can safely deduce that they made an appointment to meet, and that Charbonneau planned to kill him. Green, however, takes no chances, steals a knife, and murders Charbonneau before he knows what's going on."

Palmer was nodding the whole time. "Uh huh, I'd stake a hundred bucks, or, um, any amount of money on the fact that's just what happened. But do we have any proof?"

Two Bears grimaced. "Let's see. We've got means, Green clearly had an opportunity to steal the knife. We've got motive, Green needs to silence Charbonneau before he can bring charges against him. We've got opportunity, all right, we don't know this, but although we have no way of knowing they met out by the statue, there is no evidence that Green was in his room at the time. But proof? I don't think so."

Palmer scratched some more and said, "Maybe not, but I don't think you need proof of the murder of the younger Charbonneau. I'd be surprised if we could not find sufficient proof of the murder of his father. Kevin Charbonneau would have been collecting evidence of the murder for years. The DNA results would have only been the final proof. If you searched his office in Carson County, I'm sure you could find it. I'm not sure how to handle this. You'll have to report to Jack Hanson immediately, of course, but I'm not sure how the jurisdiction on the older charge will work. Once Green is taken in on charges of the first murder, there's a good possibility that he'll crack under interrogation and admit to the second. I guess I'd notify the F.B.I. They'd be able to work across county lines with undiminished authority."

As Two Bears was frantically taking notes, Knutson abruptly stood and said, "Congratulations, Sheriff, you have solved your first case."

Jason sadly shook his head and said, "No, I really didn't. You were the one who was able to get the story of the matching DNA. It's another Palmer Knutson murder case and the Twin Cities will have a field day."

"No, Jason, they won't. It happened in your county. Greg Refsahl called your office and talked to you first. His conversation with me was merely a question of how to proceed because he had done the testing on his own time and not notified his superiors. He'd known me for a long time and merely wanted to run it by me first. Had I not been available, he would have told you anyway. Your case, your credit, and, if you want it, a great boost to your career. As they said in the old westerns, 'My work here is done.' I'm going home."

Jason stood and almost violently shook Palmer's hand. "Right. I'll get right to work on it. We will have to track down Richard Stumpf, if he is still alive, and meet with prosecutors, but I expect that tomorrow we'll be able to arrest Harvey Green for murder. I must say, the prospect does seem almost delicious."

Ten minutes later, Palmer was out of town, driving back to his beloved Otter Tail County. Since Ellie was not in her usual seat next to him, waiting to give a grimace of distaste, he slipped a Jethro Tull CD into his Bose system. He let the sounds of Ian Anderson playing his flute in "Living in the Past" float over him. Life was good. A murder case all wrapped up by his new colleague. He could think about more pleasant things. The forecast for the weekend was good and the parade in Perham on Saturday would be well attended. He daydreamed about if his uniform was clean and pressed, he couldn't remember the last time he had worn it. He contemplated the offer he had received from a friend in Perham who loved classic cars. "Don't just ride in your usual sheriff's car," he had told Palmer. "Go for a little class. Let me drive you around in my 1955 Jaguar XK140, quite possibly the most beautiful car in the world." *What the hell,* Palmer thought. *Why not? Maybe I should also raid petty cash to toss out Tootsie Rolls to the kids. Why not?"*

The miles rolled by and soon he was passing the entrance to Itasca State Park. Could that only have been a week ago? As he thought about his busy week, he decided that there was no reason for him to go into the office for a short time in the afternoon. He justified this by reasoning the parade on Saturday was an official function, and, therefore, technically, he would be working overtime. Ellie was still down in the cities. He would have the house to himself. He had just checked the latest Minette Walters book out of the library. What could be better than to lose oneself in fine writing and imagining that Western Minnesota was really West Sussex, that Fergus Falls was really Chichester, and that Opperman Lake was really the English Channel.

CHAPTER FIFTEEN

THE *NEW YORK TIMES* CROSSWORD PUZZLE on Fridays was always difficult, but it seemed even tougher on that morning. Palmer was forced to go on the Internet to find the answers for one whole quarter of the puzzle. It left him feeling defeated. By the time he got to his office, however, he was in better spirits. Generally his office tended to cheer him up as well, since it had been accumulating the detritus of his life for more than thirty years. Like the mind of its occupant, the office was tidy. It had a U.S flag on the right and a Minnesota flag on the left. On the walls were maps of Minnesota, Otter Tail County, and Norway. Once one knew where everything was in those three places, one didn't really need to study further. To stare at him, and to remind him that work would keep his species from the door, was a wolfskin with the head attached—a treasure the worth of which Ellie and Palmer disagreed upon.

The sheriff had recently added what he considered to be another marvelous treasure to the top of his desk. It was a large globe which his daughter had somehow rescued from the dumpster of the school where she was a teacher. To be sure, it showed a united Yugoslavia and a divided Germany, but it was still a swell globe. Palmer had always wanted one. Now he sat contemplating how London was actually as far north as Winnipeg and that Fergus Falls was actually quite a ways south of Paris and that Cairo was really north of Miami. It was while he was thinking of the pyramids that Orly Peterson bounded in.

"So! Welcome back! How was the funeral?"

Palmer's mood darkened somewhat as he looked at his chief deputy. Oh, he still liked him well enough, but as he stood there in his pressed khaki uniform with dark-brown epaulets and shiny gold OTCSD letters on his collar points, Palmer felt weary. His L.A.P.D. sunglasses were pushed up on the top of his cropped brown hair and he just seemed to radiate energy. *Oh, well,* thought Palmer, *I was once young myself. At least I presume I was. I don't seem to be able to remember it.* Aloud he said, "I suppose you could say the funeral was fine. We all attended the service, heard good things about the late sheriff Charbonneau, the governor was there to look aggrieved, we had a little lunch, and we left."

"And how was your time with Jason Two Bears? Did you solve his murder case for him?"

"Actually," Palmer began, "that's quite a story, and I'll be glad to tell you all about it. I can't right now, but as soon as certain things are put in motion, I'll tell you all about it. As I said before, it's not my case and it should go through channels before I have anything to say about it."

Orly sighed inwardly and reflected, *Yep, that's Knutson. Always playing by the book. What? Does he think I'd rush out and tell people?* But he did not show that it bothered him, and said, "I heard a great joke while you were gone."

It was Knutson's turn to sigh inwardly. *Here it comes,* he thought, *another Norwegian joke.* Aloud he said, "All right, lay it on me."

Deputy Peterson was already grinning as he said, "Okay, so here's the deal. God decided on a new policy for admittance into heaven. He told St. Peter to admit anybody, without further background checks, if they had suffered through a really bad day on the day that they died. Sure enough, almost as soon as the new policy goes into effect a guy comes up to the pearly gates and St Peter says, 'Please tell me about the day you died.'

Palmer said, "Was the guy Norwegian?"

Peterson said, "How do I know? Why do you always have to have every joke be a Norwegian joke? There are other people in the world, you know."

Knutson considered slugging him in the gut.

"So anyway," Orly continued, "the guy says 'I was suspecting my wife of having an affair, that every noon hour she would bring her lover back to our twenty-eighth floor apartment. I decided I was going to catch them at it. I thought I had it timed just right and so I burst in and there was my wife, running around half naked, yelling at me and hitting me with a sofa cushion. I couldn't find him anywhere, and I was just about to give up when I thought I heard something from our balcony. Sure enough, there was a guy hanging over the edge by his fingertips. I grabbed my golf putter and mashed his fingers and he fell to the ground. I thought it served him right, but when I looked over I noticed that he had landed in some soft bushes and was still alive.' Got the picture, Palmer? Okay, so then the guy says 'Seeing that he was still alive absolutely enraged me. I ran back into the apartment, pushed our small refrigerator onto the balcony, and heaved it over the side. It fell twenty-eight stories and crushed him. However, that exertion and the general excitement of the moment was such that I almost immediately had a heart attack and died.'

"'Well,' St. Peter thought, 'it was a crime of passion, and the guy certainly did have a bad day, and who was he to question God's new policy?' So he said, "Welcome to the kingdom of heaven.' A few seconds later a second guy comes up and St. Peter asks him to tell him the detail of his day. The guy says, 'You're not going to believe this. I was on my balcony on the twenty-ninth floor of my apartment building, doing my daily exercises, when I lost my balance, stumbled over my weights, and fell over the side. I thought I was a goner until I was able to grab the railing of the balcony just beneath me. I was hanging there thinking I was saved when this man came out, swearing in a way that would make a pirate blush, and beat on my fingers. I fell all the way down but landed on some bushes that broke my fall. Just when I thought I had cheated death again, I looked up just in time to see a refrigerator crush me. There was no escape from that!'

"St. Peter was horrified. The poor sap had no luck at all and he clearly had a very bad day. He clapped him on the back and said, 'Welcome to the kingdom of heaven!'"

Palmer ostentatiously looked at his watch and said, "Do you ever get any work done in this office?"

Orly said, "Just wait, the best is yet to come. A third guy comes up and St. Peter explains the new entrance requirement and asks the guy what his last day on earth was like. The guy says, 'Okay, picture this. I'm naked and sitting in this refrigerator . . .'"

Palmer had not seen it coming. He laughed out loud, and he was soon joined by Orly. After a week of murder, it felt good to laugh. He called over to his secretary, "Hey, did you hear Orly's joke?"

"Everybody's heard Orly's joke," she replied, bored.

"Ah," thought Palmer, "it's good to be back."

Orly made a move to leave Knutson's office when the sheriff said, "Wait, I've got a job for you. Or if you don't want to do it, find someone who will. I need somebody to go to the store, or Target, or someplace, and get a few bags of candy for the parade in Perham tomorrow. The children must learn to love their local law enforcement professionals."

"To say nothing about seeking the votes of all county dentists, huh? Yeah, I'll see to it."

Five seconds later Palmer heard him say to Chuck Schulz, "Hey, Chuck. I've got a job for you."

* *

FRIDAY AFTERNOONS WERE GENERALLY QUIET. Traffic picked up on Interstate 94, with all the people from Fargo-Moorhead going off to lake cottages, but that was a job for the highway patrol. Sheriff Knutson spent some time going over the end of the month expenditures, and checking the general budget for the end of the fiscal year. He tallied up the summons served and read the latest bulletins from St. Paul. He checked through the assignments that Orly had made up for the weekend patrols. He thought about Ellie driving back from Minneapolis in the heavy traffic and decided that if she got back in time, and hadn't eaten, he'd take her out to the Jazzy Fox. In the back of his mind he was wondering when he would receive a call from Jason Two Bears. He had just about decided to call it a day when the telephone rang.

"Palmer? Jason here. There's been a new development."

Palmer could hear the tension in his friend's voice and he leaned forward into the telephone and asked, "What happened?"

"I'll start at the beginning. I brought our conjectures and evidence in to Jack Hanson at the police department. He agreed that we had grounds for at least bringing Green in for questioning. We talked to the county attorney and contacted the F.B.I. Jill Simmons agreed to meet us when we went up to take Green in. Have you met her? She reminds me a little of Clarise Starling."

"Who's that?" Palmer asked.

"Didn't you ever see *Silence of the Lambs*? That was Jody Foster's role. Anyway, a top professional all the way. At this point, I felt pretty good about everything."

"What did you find out about Richard Stumpf?"

"Who? Oh, yeah, him. The trigger-man in the killing twenty years ago. That was relatively easy. It seems he died in prison over in Wisconsin about six years ago. The good news is that there was a good record of his DNA, and when we checked out what remained of the investigation at that time, we found that there was ample DNA evidence from the crime scene that had been retained. I don't know where Charbonneau got his hair, but he must have had access to that cold case file. So, anyway, we felt pretty good about things, that we had a pretty solid case. So we met Simmons and drove up to Grundorf. We got to the sheriff's office and nobody had seen Green all day. There was nobody at his home, and his gaudy sheriff's car was gone. We went back to the sheriff's office and while we were there, some guy came in and asked what was going on up by the old logging camp. Nobody knew, so we went up there. There's just an historical marker there now, with a little road that turns off the main highway. We saw his car and got out to look for him." After a long and uncomfortable pause, Two Bears said, "We found him."

Palmer was getting just a bit impatient and he said, "Well?'

"We found him with his throat slashed and a kitchen knife sticking in his belly. There was more blood on the corpse than I have ever seen, and I imagine the scene would have looked like what we saw in Bemidji last week if the blood had not soaked into the ground. It appeared to both Jack and me that it was exactly the same M.O. as the other killing."

"Whew! Back to square one, huh?"

"Yeah, that's what we thought at first. But Simmons laid out a new possibility. You're not going to like it."

Again Palmer could sense the unease in Jason's voice. "What? What is it?"

"She's had a lot more experience in this stuff, and has studied similar events. She said that this could only be the beginning."

"Beginning? Of What?"

"She says that, because of the savagery of the killing, we might be dealing with a serial killer. If so, it is almost certainly still someone who was at that Bemidji event, and someone who has a hatred for sheriffs."

"Your're not trying to tell me that . . ."

"Yeah, Palmer, without trying to be melodramatic, you could be next. Watch yourself. Meanwhile, I'm going to be calling all those other sheriffs and put them on their guard. This is not, I repeat, is not, to be taken lightly!"

As Palmer hung up the telephone, he noticed that his hand was shaking.

Chapter Sixteen

P ALMER STARED AT THE TELEPHONE. He knew that the proper thing to do was to notify everyone in the office that a potential threat existed. But the more he thought about it, the less he believed that he was in any danger. Besides, it was the weekend. Why would he want to make everybody worry about him? *Perhaps I should tell Orly,* he thought, *but if I did, and not tell anyone else, then everyone else would think I didn't trust them. When it comes right down to it, the whole thing is ridiculous. A serial killer of county sheriffs! Utter nonsense!* He decided to go home.

But as he took three strides toward the door, he hesitated. Perhaps he should take some precautions. He went back to his desk and unlocked the bottom drawer where he kept his thirty-eight-caliber revolver. He couldn't even remember the last time he had shot the damn thing. If ever he needed protection, however, this might be the time. He brought it out, found some bullets, and began to put the holster on. *Wait a minute,* he thought. *If I put this thing on now, without my uniform, it will look horribly out of place. If I walk out packing heat everyone will know something's up. Besides, the chances of shooting myself in the foot are probably greater than being able to use it to defend myself. Charbonneau was armed with a knife. Green never went anywhere without his gun. To hell with it! Nobody is trying to kill me.* He put the gun back and locked the drawer.

Nevertheless, as he left the building, he looked from side to side. As he walked to his car, he glanced behind the bushes. Before he entered his Acura, he checked the back seat. Ten minutes later he was home, a two-storey wooden house with a brick front. As he used his remote to open the garage door, the thought occurred to him, "Anyway, I'm sure glad I remembered to lock the house this morning. Sometimes, when Ellie goes away, I forget that. Or, did I really remember to do it?"

For a few seconds, Palmer sat in the car staring into the rear view mirror. Nobody seemed to have followed him. He was now becoming almost certain that he had failed to lock the front door that morning. He cautiously entered the house. Everything looked the same. He took a deep breath and went to check the front door. It was locked after all. He opened it and looked out. Again, there was nothing to be seen. And yet. He tried to tell himself that that he was being silly, but he seemed compelled to just check every room. He went upstairs first, and found himself actually panting by the time he had climbed the fourteen steps. He refused to consider that he was becoming anxious, he must really be out of shape. He went into his son's room, going so far as to check the closet. He hadn't looked in there for years. A boy-scout shirt was still hanging there, and clearly had not been disturbed since Trygve had last been home.

A search of his daughter's rooms and the master bedroom revealed that nothing was out of place. He began to berate himself for being paranoid. He returned downstairs and went through the dining room, the family room, and the kitchen. There was nothing unusual about the downstairs or the upstairs. "I suppose," he said to himself, "I should check the basement just to be on the safe side."

He walked down and glanced under the ping-pong table. "Nobody hiding under there," he chuckled to himself. He went into the utility room and peered behind furnace. He glanced through the storage room and made sure that no one could be hiding amongst the Christmas decorations. He breathed deeply, and then he heard it. It sounded like the front door had just opened!

He went back to the storage room and saw his long neglected golf bag. Taking the first club he found, he noticed that it was his "trusty three iron." It had been more than three years since Palmer had played golf. He looked at the face of the Spalding club and noticed that there was still dried grass on it. For just a second, he felt a bit ashamed that he had put it away in such a condition, then held it up to his eye and muttered, "You always failed me before, but Three Iron, don't fail me now." And then, "My God, I'm cracking up! I'm talking to a golf club." When he had checked it earlier, the lock on the door seemed just as it should be. Had he failed to lock it again? If not . . .

Terror began to take over logic. He remembered how he felt when someone attempted to blast him away with a shotgun. It had been so totally unexpected that the fear only began after it was all over. This, it appeared, was just beginning. It was cool in the basement, but sweat was pouring off of him as he climbed the stairs with his three-iron ready to strike. He wished he had taken his gun. Even under these conditions, he thought, "I suppose I was never any better with a gun in my hand than I was with golf club."

He cautiously pushed the door open with the golf club. As he peaked through the half open doorway, he had a line of sight to the front door. He gasped as he noticed that it was indeed open. More than likely he had not closed it firmly enough. Perhaps the wind had blown it open. Or maybe the wind had nothing to do with it. He crept forward and silently locked it. He slowly climbed the stairs, listening to his own breathing. Once again, he examined each bedroom, each bathroom, and each closet. He even found himself looking under each bed, even though he realized that, at seven inches off the ground, it would take a very small assassin to

hide in such a place. On the ground floor, he searched behind every chair, and looked in every closet. He even looked
under the sink. At last he began to chuckle, to laugh at his
own paranoia. He filled a tumbler with ice and had a long
drink of water. Then the thought occurred to him. "Perhaps
one could have sneaked down into the basement while I
was upstairs." Gripping the golf club firmly again, he began
his descent, for some reason more anxious now than ever.

There was no one there. There had never been anyone
there. Palmer allowed common sense to return and realized
that he must not have closed the door all the way in the first
place. But the whole experience had left him shattered. He
considered finding a beer, or maybe even making himself a
gin and tonic. He could just sit out on the patio and chill out.
But then the thought occurred to him that just because the
killer had used a knife on the first two sheriffs, there was
no guarantee the he would not use a scoped deer rifle on
the third. The house, his home for almost thirty years, no
longer felt quite so safe. He decided to go "home."

CHAPTER SEVENTEEN

PALMER CLIMBED BACK INTO HIS ACURA and headed out of town. About twelve miles away, near the town of Underwood, was a two-acre plot of ground that had been the cradle of Palmer Knutson. Perhaps it was not the original site of the Garden of Eden, but, to Palmer, the two locations must have been similar. Palmer tried the radio with its classic rock station. However marvelous Led Zeppelin was, with Page and Plant at their very best, he just couldn't get in the mood. He tried a CD of French Impressionism. Too dreamy. He turned on the Minnesota Public Radio news station and started to listen to *All Things Considered*. He couldn't concentrate. Finally, he found the Minnesota Public Radio classical music station. It was playing Handel's "Hail the Conquering Hero" from Judas Maccabeas. Fantastic. Something that could take his mind off murder and threats of murder!

There was little left of the Knutson residence. Once there had been a barn, a granary, a chicken coop, a hog house, a machine shed, a two-holer out-house, and a farm home, all protected by a shelterbelt of box elders. Now, the only indication that it had once been a place of residence and agricultural commerce was a tall windmill, a straggly line of trees, and a small stand of lilac bushes. When Palmer's father had retired, he rented the land to a neighbor, and when he died, and Palmer's mother had moved to the nursing home, the land was sold. The new owner naturally wanted to farm his property as efficiently as possible, and so one by one the buildings were torn down and burned. At last, only the house was left, and that too was removed. It had been taken to another farmstead and was now housing wheat instead of children. Yet, to Palmer Knutson, it was always a place of solace and contemplation.

He parked the car on the driveway, fearing that the deep ruts from generations of wagons would make the passage of a twenty-first-century automobile risky. It was so quiet, he thought, and no one could ever really know where he was. Nevertheless, such was the nature of his mental state that he looked both ways down the road and eyed the lilac bush suspiciously. No, he decided, nobody could possibly be hiding there. He was home. He was safe.

He walked through the tall grass until he reached the hole in the ground where his house used to be. After the house had been removed, all that remained was a concrete lined hole in the ground. Over the years, the new owner had used this as his own private stone dump. Every year, because of the freezing and thawing nature of Minnesota winters, field-stones work their way to the surface. They were especially common in the Park Region area, and, unless picked, could do real damage to modern farm machinery. The pile had grown since the last time Palmer had been out there.

It was a glorious late afternoon. The temperature was in the low eighties and there was only a light breeze. It was one of the few times that Palmer had returned when he did not hear the mournful wail of the windmill as the blades turned around their ungreased axle. In fact, it was almost unnaturally quiet. From a distance he could hear the occasional moo of cattle and from the box elder grove, a lone crow was warning him not to come any closer. He found a smooth stone and sat, trying not to think about a cold steel blade running across his throat.

He had a brief fascination with the attempt of an ant, laden with some delicious ort, to climb the steep side of a rock, then Palmer looked up to see a new friend. It was a little gold-and-black "striped gopher." Technically, he reminded himself, it was a "thirteen-lined ground squirrel," or, to be more exact, it was a *spermophilus tridecemlineatus.*" For some reason, he remembered that from a report he had been forced to do in high school biology class. His biology teacher, who was also, unfortunately, his football coach, had decided to teach Palmer a lesson about discipline. Palmer had been wallowing in the glory of the last Rose Bowl appearance of the Minnesota Golden Gophers when he should have been dissecting a frog. "Of the phylum *chordate,*" Palmer now said aloud. His little friend stood straight up, as immovable as a stick, and stared at him. Uncomfortably, as Palmer stared at him, he remembered the time in third grade when he and his classmates had found a gopher hole, organized a relay of water in peach cans from the nearby slough, and tried to drown out a gopher just like that. When he came out, they had chased the poor thing around with baseball bats. He did not remember whether they ever hit it, and now hoped that they had not.

Perhaps the life of a gopher should inspire me, Palmer thought. *After all, they only run around for six months out of the year. The rest of the time, they hibernate. Six months of sleeping. Hard to beat that life! I wonder who solves their crimes? One would hope that a gopher sheriff would be more perceptive than me. I still can't believe the difference in Ellie's testimony and mine. Why does she see things that I don't, things that are right in front of my face?*

Palmer began to contemplate what he had read in Ellie's report, not only the facts presented, but also the inferences she made from those facts. He concentrated on each of the people in the Radisson ballroom that night, and what he had read and seen during the last week. One by one he mentally sorted the suspects into what he knew about them, and what he could then surmise. Had their behavior changed since the night of the murder until the funeral of Kevin Charbonneau. How did they interact with him and with each other? Could one of them conceivably be a serial killer? It made his head hurt. Suddenly, the little gopher scurried away. What had spooked him?

Palmer realized that he had scared him, when he had merely shifted his weight because he was getting stiff. It had been a simple non-threatening move, but to Goldie the Gopher, it had meant something. Something was starting to click in Palmer's mind. Yes, it was what Ellie had suggested in her testimony. It could tie into what he had seen at the funeral. And if that were so, then . . .

Somehow, speculation turned into certainty. It was certainty without proof, but if Jason Two Bears and that F.B.I. agent were skilled interrogators, that might not be that much of an obstacle. A confession? Better than proof! The absolute stillness of the summer evening was disturbed by a cell phone conversation between the sheriff of Otter Tail County and a sheriff in far off Bemidji.

Chapter Eighteen

P ALMER WAS ABLE TO PERSUADE ELLIE to come along with him for the Perham parade because he always considered her to be a prime political asset. He drove the Otter Tail County Sheriff's Office car to Perham, but was finally convinced to ride in his friend's Jaguar. It was a beautifully restored car, with silver paint and a tan interior. He talked Ellie into sitting in the passenger seat while he propped himself on the roof cover and held his legs between the driver and Ellie. Resplendent in his uniform, he had a magnificent vantage point to see potential voters and to toss candy to the kids.

There is something majestic and All-American about a parade in a small Minnesota town. All the businesses in town had a float or a vintage car, and most of them threw prodigious handfuls of candy to eager children. There were queens and junior princesses representing every pageant in the northwestern part of the state, most of them wearing a somewhat dim continence as they waved to no one in particular. And there were bands. The Perham Yellow Jackets band looked smart as they played Sousa's *Sempre Fidelis* march, and most of the crowd applauded. The neighboring town of Frazee, not as large as Perham, ably represented the Hornets with a rocking rendition of the "Hey Song," and the rest of the crowd applauded. Along the path, politicians, eager to win a vote for state representative or county attorney, passed out campaign literature and affixed stickers with their name in gaudy colors on the shirts of the willing. Most people, to be polite, accepted the literature and soon deposited it, unread, in a waste barrel.

It was a glorious June morning, and throngs of "lake people" had come in from their cottages to enjoy the spectacle. As Palmer rode by, waving to people he knew and targeting his candy to the little kids—and attempting as far as possible to exclude the greedy big kids who had shown up with buckets—polite applause broke out. It was fun. He enjoyed the crowd, he enjoyed the children, he enjoyed the sun, and he enjoyed the Jaguar. And yet.

The solution to the double murders in the wake of the sheriffs' conference gnawed at him. When he had presented his theories to Jason Two Bears the previous evening, he was pleased to find that Jason agreed with him. The acting Sheriff of Beltrami County was going to contact his counterpart in the Bemidji Police Department and the F.B.I. and make an arrest. Jason had promised to inform him of the latest developments. He had not. Had something gone wrong?

At last the parade was over, the local riding clubs and horse teams had, as usual, brought up the rear, thus avoiding the necessity of forcing the bands to watch their step. Palmer and Ellie met with old friends and made new ones, and decided to have lunch at the Station House. They decided to leave the scheduled events of the rest of the day for those younger and more enthusiastic, and drove back home to their beloved Fergus Falls. On the way, Palmer said, "It is such a beautiful day. You know, I've been feeling a little guilty because of the way I left Orly out of the loop on this Bemidji case. We haven't had them over since he and Allysha got married. It's a beautiful day and we have those sirloin steaks in the freezer. I really haven't done any grilling since the snow melted. What say we ask them over for supper tonight?"

Ellie considered this. "Well, since you kept the house so clean when I was gone, that would be no problem. I could make a nice fresh salad, and . . . Yes, why don't you give them a call."

When they got home, Palmer changed out of his uniform and put on shorts, a tee shirt, and his Nikes. He had not had a chance to tackle the Saturday crossword puzzle, and it was time to face that ultimate challenge. As he picked up his pen, however, Ellie, said, "Weren't you going to call up Orly and Allysha and ask them over?"

Palmer got up and got his cell phone. "Oh, yah, I forgot about that. But you know, I'm surprised that Jason Two Bears hasn't called. I expected him to call this morning, and that is why I had my cell phone with me at all times. I hope there haven't been any problems."

Ellie said, "Are you sure the battery on that thing is charged?"

Palmer looked at her with contempt. "Of course it's charged. Do you really think I wouldn't have checked that? Give me some credit."

Ellie shrugged and said, "Let me see that thing a second."

Palmer sighed and handed it over.

"You know, dear, I've always found that a cell phone works best when it is turned on."

"What! Let me see! Oh, *heste fies*! (An odd Norwegian expression for the flatulence of a horse.) How could I be such a dolt!" Knutson quickly turned on the cell phone and discovered several calls from Orly Peterson and six messages from Jason Two Bears. The messages from Jason were virtually identical. "Arrest made. Have a confession. Call me ASAP." Palmer said, "I'm going up to my office. If anybody calls here, tell 'em I'm on my way."

* *

As Palmer walked into the Otter Tail County Law Enforcement Center, Orly spotted him coming up the stairway. "Where have you been? Everybody's been trying to get ahold of you. Did you hear that Harvey Green was found murdered yesterday? Oh, and nice uniform, by the way."

Palmer led him into his office and as he sat down and drew the telephone closer said, "Yes, I found that out yesterday."

"Well, why didn't you tell me? I heard he was killed in exactly the same way as that Charbonneau. I got to thinking, hey, that could be the start of something serious, maybe even a serial killer targeting sheriffs. I've been worried about you."

Palmer impatiently waved his hand in the air and said, "Yah, I know. I suppose I should have told you. I'm sorry. I'll explain everything, but first I gotta call Jason Two Bears.

Orly could only hear Palmer's side of the conversation. "Jason. Palmer Knutson here . . . Yah, I know. It seems my cell phone wasn't working." Orly thought Palmer looked nervous as he said that. "What happened? . . . Ah, good. No problems with the arrest? . . . No resistance of any kind, huh . . . Well, I didn't think there would be . . . So what's next? . . . Uh huh . . . Uh huh . . . Uh huh . . . Yep . . . and tell Jack Hanson or Jill Simmons and anybody at the F.B.I. that they can call me if they have any questions . . . Okay, then. Good work. Talk to you later. Goodbye."

Palmer sighed and leaned back in his chair. "I don't suppose since it's Saturday that anybody bothered to make any coffee? Oh, well, I suppose we can get by. Oh, and before I forget it, Ellie and I would like to ask if you and Allysha would like to come over for steaks tonight. I thought I'd fire up the grill and we can have a nice gin and tonic while I burn 'em."

Orly smiled. "That sounds nice. I'll check with my bride. I'm sure we'd love to come. But on one condition! You've gotta tell me what's been going on and what that telephone conversation was all about."

"It's a deal. Are you sure there isn't any coffee around?"

Orly said, "Just a minute. I've got something even better." A short time later he returned carrying two bottles of cold beer.

"Where did you get that?" Palmer asked suspiciously, looking around to make sure no one had seen Orly come into the room.

"Chuck Schultz confiscated this from an inebriated speed boat driver. He came back and put it in the lunchroom refrigerator, with the belief that he was preserving evidence. Of course, he didn't log it in, and the guy's already paid the fine, so I don't know what else we would do with it. Skol!"

CHAPTER NINETEEN

"B RILLIANT! SKOL YOURSELF!" PALMER REPLIED and took a long pull on the bottle. "All right, I'll start from the beginning. I must say, this is one of the nastiest cases I've ever been involved with. I say 'involved with' because it has never been our case at all. So, you know how Charbonneau was murdered under the Paul Bunyan statue in Bemidji. It was soon discovered that the murder weapon came from the carving cart used by the Radisson Hotel staff on the night of the banquet. Furthermore, evidence seemed to indicate that it must have been taken by one of ten people who rode out the storm in the ballroom. Now, I knew I didn't take it, I was reasonably sure Ellie didn't take it, and, although possible, it was unlikely that the murder victim took it. That left seven people. Jack Hanson, of the Bemidji Police Department, and Jason Two Bears, acting sheriff of Beltrami County, worked together to interview all of us who there were that night. After taking our testimony, we were allowed to leave.

"I gotta admit, I gave the whole thing some thought, and I couldn't see any way any of those seven people could have murdered Charbonneau. Means? Well, that was obvious, the carving knife, but I certainly didn't see anybody take it. Opportunity? Basically, anybody who didn't have an iron clad alibi could have met Charbonneau under the statues. Motive? That's what stumped me. Why would anyone want to kill a young sheriff. I mean, he'd hardly had time to make enemies. Then Jason Two Bears called me up and asked me to go over the transcripts of those interviews. It was here that I discovered two things. The first is that my wife makes the best witness I've ever seen. Her observations and her interpretations were vital to solving this case. I told her so last night when I unraveled the case for her. I think she was pleased.

"Anyhow, the second thing I discovered was that her observations made it clear that Kevin Charbonneau tended to play mind games with people. She said it was almost as though he were setting them up for blackmail. Furthermore, she noticed an especially intense interaction between Green and Charbonneau. What this was, of course, she had no way of knowing. The question then was which of those people had a secret so dangerous that they were willing to kill for it. According to Ellie, while the others might have been upset or nervous—there was, after all, a danger that everyone would be sucked up into the sky by a tornado—it was the interaction between Green and Charbonneau that seemed most contentious. If for no other reason, then, Green would seem to be the most likely suspect."

Palmer stopped to take another gulp of beer. "I hope nobody saw you bring this in here. The public would not like it. Anyway, as I was saying, we had absolutely nothing to go on here. Then, in a development totally unrelated to what Hanson and Two Bears were looking into, Jason gets a call from a technologist from the B.C.A. laboratory in Bemidji. It seems a few weeks ago Charbonneau brought in two DNA samples and asked him to see if they matched. This guy, who grew up in Fergus Falls, by the way, agreed to test the samples in complete confidence. He didn't even tell his supervisors. When he found out that Charbonneau had been murdered, he did the right thing and notified Two Bears. It turned out that the DNA, on both samples, came from a guy named Richard Stumpf. The name meant nothing to either Jason or me, but it turns out that this guy was a prime suspect in the murder of Kevin Charbonneau's father. At the time of the murder, about twenty years ago, he had the perfect alibi in that he was supposed to have been locked up in Harvey Green's jail. The conclusion was obvious. Since no one benefited from the murder of the elder Charbonneau other than the Green family, Kevin Charbonneau had discovered that Harvey Green arranged for this Stumpf character to murder his father. He lets Stumpf out of jail and Stumpf obliges him by murdering old man Charbonneau. Last week, on the night of the murder, Charbonneau arranged to meet Green by the Paul Bunyan statue. He came prepared. Something that was not released to the public was that Charbonneau carried a rather deadly hunting knife. Whether or not he was actually planning to kill Green, well, I guess we'll never know.

"So, Charbonneau meets Green, but Green, thanks to Charbonneau's broad hints made in the ballroom during the storm, knows what's up and decides to silence Charbonneau. Obvious conclusion, right? Jason Two Bears and an F.B.I. agent went to arrest Green. Even if there was no direct evidence connecting him with the murder of the younger Charbonneau, there was certainly evidence to charge him with the elder.

"Well, you heard what happened to Green. The *modus operendi* was identical to the killing of Charbonneau, leading to that nonsense about a serial killing. Again, I do apologize for not informing you about all this. But, in fact, you reacted just as I feared you would. I did recognize that it could be a serial killing, but it seemed unlikely, and I just thought if I kept it to myself, I wouldn't spoil other people's weekend. The most obvious question would be, if the murders were not committed by the same individual, how could they be so identical? The answer, of course, is that it could be a copycat murder, but this would mean that whoever committed the second murder had access to all of the information on the first murder. Who could get that? Again, obviously, somebody involved in law enforcement, particularly someone with a direct interest in the case . . . Or, his wife.

"When I was reading the transcript of Ellie's interview, I noticed she kept referring to Alan Sorgren's nervous conduct, and even suggested that it looked like he was on something. There were references to methamphetamines during that conversation when everyone was looking at the sky. Even I remember that. Then, when we were all gathered at the funeral, I noticed Harvey Green come up to Alan Sorgren and Sorgren seemed very glad to see him. I thought Green had a rather obnoxious smug look on his face as he seemed to slip something in Sorgren's pocket. But at the time, I made no connection.

"I was thinking about this last night and for some reason I remembered that little scene between Sorgren and Green at the funeral. I called Jason and suggested that he look into possible meth use by Alan Sorgren, something previously suggested by Neil Meyer. Sorgren would have known all the particulars about how Charbonneau was murdered and could have done a copycat. Jason and Jill Simmons, the F.B.I. agent, went out to talk to him. Instead, they talked to his wife, Carla Sorgren. The day after the funeral, Carla had checked her husband into that Hazeltine rehabilitation center down by the cities. She received a call a few hours later telling her that the staff at Hazeltine had found significant quantities of methamphetamines that Alan had tried to smuggle into the center, believing, apparently, that he could wean himself off the stuff gradually. Now, Carla knew that Alan did not have any of that stuff for the few days before the funeral. It was obvious that Harvey Green had supplied the junk right there at the church. She knew all about how Charbonneau was killed—other than Alan's use of meth they seem not to have had many secrets between each other—and she decided that as long as Green was around he would keep Alan addicted.

"According to Jason, when they discovered that Alan had gone into rehab, and could not possibly have murdered Green, they casually asked Carla Sorgren if she had murdered Green. She responded rather coolly that she had. They arrested her and she is now in custody. So, therefore, I am not in danger of being filleted by a serial killer."

"That's a relief," Orly said. "How do you feel about that?"

"I must admit to being relieved myself. Now, hide these bottles and let's go home. Unless we hear differently, we'll see you and Allysha at about, say, six?"

Orly left and Palmer was alone in his office. He looked around at the comforting items in his office, the mementos and curiousities that seemed to have gathered over the past few years. Although the case had involved the death of two of his colleagues, he felt a satisfaction that the case had been solved, and he turned his mind to the pleasantness of the Perham parade and the anticipation of the sirloin steaks. He was on his way out of the door when the telephone rang.

"Palmer? This is Jason. I just called to tell you about what just happened. I thought you might find it interesting. I just got a call from the chairman of the board of the Beltrami County Commission. He said that they were holding their usual meeting on Monday and wanted me to be there. He said that they had all informally agreed that they wanted to take the "acting" part of my title away. So, I guess you can just call me the sheriff of Beltrami County."

"That's great, Jason," Palmer said, "I'm so glad you called to tell me. See what happens when you "let your light so shine among men?"